Horatio's One Wish

Horatio's One Wish

By Joshua Kriesberg

Illustrations by James Bernardin

Horatio's One Wish

Published by Blue Bog Press

ISBN-10: 0988696703
ISBN-13: 978-0-9886967-0-9

Cover and interior illustrations: James Bernardin
Book design: Magdalena Bassett, www.bassettstudio.com

For Max and Benjamin

Table of Contents

N
S
E
W
HORATIO'S BURROW
WINGWOTS' ROCK
FOREST OF EPOH
GLOB SWAMP
LATCH'S HOUSE
SWIMMING HOLE
TOURNAMENT OF ARCHERS
SCREECH FOREST
GREAT BLUE BOG
SCARRETCHEN'S LAIR
WISHING STONES
HEDGEHOG VILLAGE

Chapter 1

Horatio and Rollic

You never think someone you see almost every day for seven years would disappear one day and not come back. But that's what happened to Horatio when his best friend, Rollic, went exploring downriver.

On that morning, Horatio lounged on the grass at the edge of the riverbank, letting the sun warm his belly and the water cool his feet. He drifted along with the clouds above him and entered the dreamy state hedgehogs may fall into when there's no threat of a predator about.

Something tugged lightly on his left foot under the water. "A little fish?" thought Horatio. Then something yanked his right foot. "That's no fish." He sat up and peered into the river.

A spray of water hit him full in the face. "Rollic!" He sputtered at the otter. Horatio was delighted to see him.

"Hi, Horatio. Whatcha doing?"

"Nothing much. Just lying in the sun."

Rollic dived under the water, and a few seconds later sprung up and loped onto the riverbank. He gave himself two hard shakes; the cool spray hit Horatio in the face again.

"Sure is a nice day today," Rollic said, as he lay on his back. He rested his front white paws on his silky brown stomach. He was the only otter around who had white paws, but it didn't bother him.

"Uh-huh," Horatio let out a deep breath. The summer weather almost always seemed agreeable to Horatio. Even when it rained, it seemed to rain only enough to cool things down or to moisten things up.

Rollic jumped back to his feet. He sensed something. He paced along the riverbank, his head bobbed up and down, his black nose twitched, and in a flash he dived in. A moment later he popped his head out of the water, dangling a fish in his mouth. He let the flow of the river take him, like the wind whisking up a leaf and gently setting it back down again. Effortlessly, Rollic glided to a rock in the middle of the river and climbed aboard.

"U want um," he called to Horatio, the fish clutched in his mouth.

Horatio laughed and shook his head. Horatio was a mushroom-and-berry kind of creature. Rollic, on the other hand, loved his fish.

Rollic slid off the rock and swam back to the riverbank. He dropped the fish on the grass. "Should I save it for later?" Rollic grinned. It was a long-standing joke between them. Rollic didn't save *anything* for later.

The fish gasped, its tail flopping wildly. Rollic put a paw on it to hold it down. Horatio stared at the fish gasping for air, as if it were mouthing the words, "Don't. Don't." Horatio looked away.

"Are you sure I shouldn't save it?" Rollic teased Horatio. Rollic found Horatio's squeamishness amusing. He held his mouth wide open above the fish, his sharp teeth gleaming, goading Horatio to watch. Horatio knew better than to take the bait.

Horatio tried to go back to staring at the clouds, but the chewing, slurping, and gulping noises prevented him from returning to that dreamy state he had been in before.

"That hit the spot," said Rollic—bits of fish still clinging to his whiskers. He dunked his head in the river and cleaned his face off with his paws.

Horatio plucked a mushroom he'd been lying on and pondered what to do with it.

"Well?" asked Rollic.

Horatio flipped the mushroom in the air and caught it. "I think I'll save it for later."

"Ha! I knew it! I knew you'd save it!" Rollic spun himself in a circle before settling back down on the grass. "Hey, Horatio, I heard there's a cool swimming hole. I'm going to check it out today. It's pretty far downriver. Past that waterfall that nearly got me last time."

Even though Rollic was a young pup, he was almost fully grown, and his family let him explore the river, as long as he came back before dark. Rollic could use the river to take him places far from where Horatio lived, places Horatio only knew about by the stories Rollic told him.

"I can't believe I survived that waterfall," Rollic began. Horatio had heard the waterfall story often, but he enjoyed listening to it almost as much as Rollic enjoyed retelling it. "There I was, swimming along. The current was getting stronger, but I wasn't worried. I told myself to grab hold of the big rock I was heading toward, but then the current pulled me right past it. There was nothing else to grab on to. Nothing! The current kept getting stronger. The river kept getting wider. Too wide for me to make it to shore. I tried to swim upstream but couldn't. Suddenly, I was tumbling right over the waterfall. I must have fallen a hundred feet. Hit a rock coming down. Thought I was a goner. I went way, way underwater. When I finally came up, I was completely spent. I barely made it back to shore. If I had hit my head, I would have been dead for sure."

"You were lucky."

"Yeah, my mom and dad were so upset when I got back," said Rollic, grinning sheepishly.

Unlike Rollic, Horatio had lived by himself along the riverbank, for as long as he could remember. He didn't know where he had been born or who his parents were or even who raised him when he was smaller. He presumed that was the way the world was—otters live with their families, and hedgehogs don't.

"Rollic, what's it like to have parents?"

"Parents? They always like to tell you what to do. And what *not* to do." Rollic stopped. He could tell Horatio needed a real answer. He thought for a while. Then he said quietly, "They're like the river."

Horatio understood. The river meant everything to river otters.

"But I envy you," Rollic went on to say.

"Me? Why would you envy me?"

"You don't have to take orders from anyone. You're so . . ." he tried to find the right word, ". . . self-reliant."

That comment almost made Horatio laugh out loud.

He felt certain he would rather have his parents and be part of a family than be so self-reliant.

"Well, I better get going," said Rollic, hopping to his feet. "I'm not sure how long it will take for me to get to this swimming hole, and I don't want to come home too late—or my folks will really kill me," he winked.

"Okay, I'll see you when you get back."

Rollic dropped into the water, twirled onto his back, and waved good-bye as he floated down the river.

Horatio waved back, feeling ever more earthbound the farther Rollic floated away.

Rollic twirled again, waved once more, and dropped out of sight.

Chapter 2

Horatio's Journey Begins

Horatio sat straight up with a jolt. A fear about Rollic had jerked him awake in the middle of the night. His heart raced. Rollic hadn't stopped by on his way back yesterday. Had something happened to him? "Perhaps he was late and needed to get home before dark. Everything will be fine tomorrow. I need some sleep." But the fear wouldn't leave him. He tossed and turned for hours.

Near dusk the next day Horatio saw a floating shape come up the river. He could tell it was an otter, but it swam heavier and slower than Rollic did. As it came closer, Horatio could see it was Rollic's older brother.

He called out to Horatio, "Have you seen Rollic lately?"

"I saw him yesterday morning. Haven't seen him since."

"That's the last time we saw him, too. Did he say where he was going?"

"He was going to visit a swimming hole."

"Yeah, I was just there. No sign of him." His face became despondent. "If you see him, will you tell him to come home? We're all worried about him."

"Of course."

"Thanks."

Rollic's older brother floated on his back, waved a paw, then twirled and went underwater.

"Rollic said good-bye the same way," Horatio thought.

Horatio stood for the longest time at the edge of the riverbank hoping he might see the small figure of Rollic swimming upriver in the distance. The power and immensity of the river—the way it thundered and bubbled, gurgled and churned—always filled Horatio with awe. But the more he stood there waiting, scanning the river, the more futile it seemed to wait any longer. A deep feeling of loneliness swept over him. Horatio couldn't picture life without Rollic. "He's the only friend I've got."

That night Horatio had a glum dinner of mushroom and mint-leaf stew. He went to bed early. As he lay awake in bed, he heard the roar of the river deep inside him. Not the up close roar of the river he heard standing on the riverbank. It was a distant, urgent rumble, like the rapid beating of a heart. Where it came from, he couldn't tell. He sat up in bed and listened to it. He suddenly had an eerie sense the sound was Rollic calling to him, somehow, through the distance. "I hear you." Horatio whispered back. "Where are you?" But he could hear nothing more than the rapid rush of the current inside him.

"No, no, I must be imagining this," he told himself.

Horatio had another fitful night's sleep. When he awoke the next morning, he didn't hear the sound of the river at first. He took a deep breath, "I was imagining it." But as soon as he exhaled, the sound of the river came roaring back. It was as if Rollic were saying in that churning drone, "So you're awake. Good. Now hear me!"

"It *is* him. It has to be. Something's happened to him." Horatio hopped out of bed to put on his pants. "I must leave at once." Horatio hesitated. He wondered whether he should first go upriver to tell Rollic's family. But it would take him in the opposite direction. Besides, he didn't know exactly where they lived or how far away. "No, he might be hurt. I have no time to waste."

He packed his whole supply of mushrooms and berries into his knapsack. Across the top flap of his knapsack, in large curly red letters, was the name *Horatio*, encircled by stars. One star, at the top of the circle, was larger and brighter than the others and had an arrow shooting through it. The knapsack was his one connection to those who looked after him when he was little. He took comfort knowing that at one time, when he was much younger, someone had made this knapsack and had cared enough about him to embroider his name and surround it with stars. Other than the clothes he wore and his supply of food, the knapsack was the only thing Horatio owned.

Horatio set off heading south, downriver. He stopped for a moment to take one last look at his burrow in the distance. "Will I really be able to find him? Will I be able to find my way back home, if I don't?" He shook his head, "This is no time for doubts." He dashed onward.

He kept up a steady run, on two legs, until the grass became so thick and tall, he had to fight his way through it. He found himself in a sea of grass, with no visibility beyond the blades in front of him. He came eye to eye with a beetle, clawing its way through the grass, its pinchers chomping furiously. Horatio didn't know how to speak to a beetle, but they acknowledged each other with a slight nod as they passed by.

Horatio at last burst through the dense grass into a clearing along the riverbank. He gulped in huge breaths, as if he'd been underwater all this time and had only now come up for air. He had no idea how far he had traveled, but he was relieved to see he was still heading downriver.

Horatio pressed on. He noticed a patch of fur on the ground. At first he thought some animal had been shedding. More chunks of fur spread out around him. Then he saw a sight that made him freeze—it was a

lone dismembered paw. The animal had been attacked, wounded for sure, perhaps even killed.

The sight of the poor animal's paw, the heavy warmth of the sun, and the hard slog through the grass all took their toll. Horatio finally stopped to rest. The steady drone of the river inside him continued.

He set his knapsack beside a large pointed rock on the riverbank. He lowered his face to the river and drank.

"Is that a baby porcupine down by the water?" Horatio heard a small voice ask.

"That's not a baby porcupine. I think it's a hedgehog."

Horatio jumped up. "Are they talking about me?"

"A hedgehog? Can't be. What would a hedgehog be doing here?"

"Are you a hedgehog or a baby porcupine?" a voice called to him.

"Who's there?" he whispered.

"We're up here."

"Where?" Horatio scanned the sky.

"Behind you, up here on the rock."

There, high on the rock, were dozens of the most extraordinary winged creatures he had ever seen. They had arms, and legs, and expressive faces with eyes and mouths that opened and shut like his, but their bodies were no longer than a butterfly's and fuzzy like a caterpillar's. Their hands and feet, shaped like cups, kept them suctioned to the rock. But most amazing of all, connected to their arms were wings—gray like the rock on one side and bright golden yellow on the other, so when they flapped them, the rock became illuminated, the way the river sparkles as the sun sets.

"Can you actually *talk*?" Horatio asked.

"Of course, we can." They spoke so clearly, Horatio almost stepped back and fell into the water.

"What kind of creatures are you?"

"We're Wingwots."

"I've never seen Wingwots before."

"Well, we've never seen a hedgehog in this area either," said one of the Wingwots. "You're a hedgehog, right?"

"That's right"

"See, I told you he wasn't a baby porcupine."

"Do you ever fly upriver from here?" asked Horatio.

"Certainly, we fly all over."

"But why haven't I seen you before?"

"We fly so high you can't see us. And we only land at certain spots, like this rock. This is one of our rendezvous spots. We all return to this spot to make sure everyone is accounted for."

"I see."

"What's your name?"

"Horatio."

"So Horatio, what brings a young hedgehog like you alone to these parts?"

"I'm looking for my friend, Rollic. He's an otter. He's been missing for the past couple of days."

"Where was he going?"

"To visit a swimming hole. He said lots of animals go there."

"Do your parents know where you are?" asked one Wingwot, who seemed older to Horatio, perhaps because his wings were not quite as bright.

"I don't have any parents."

"Do the folks you live with know?"

"I live by myself."

"By yourself? All by yourself?" another Wingwot interjected. "How do you fend for yourself? Protect yourself from predators?"

"What's a predator?" asked Horatio, which sent the whole group of Wingwots into a titter. They all looked at him even more intently now.

"A predator is an animal that eats other animals," one Wingwot explained. "Why, an otter is a predator! A predator of fish."

"Oh, I know that," Horatio sighed. "But no animals eat hedgehogs," he tried to reassure them.

"You've never encountered a predator your whole entire life?"

"Of me? No, of course not. I've seen Rollic eat fish before."

"Hedgehogs have many types of predators," explained a chubby Wingwot, whose fuzzy frame was much rounder in the middle. "Weasels who hide in the grass. Hawks who attack from the sky. There are foxes and ferrets, eagles and ospreys, even snapping turtles. Any one of them would eat a small mammal like you for lunch or dinner. Maybe even for breakfast—or a late morning snack on a hot day, that sort of thing."

"You're going to frighten the poor fellow," said the older Wingwot.

Horatio felt himself get queasy. "There aren't any of these predators around here, are there?"

"Oh yes, they live all around, so you have to stay hidden."

"Stay alert."

"Keep out of open fields."

"Try not to make too much noise."

"Stay downwind of them."

"Don't swim in the river."

Horatio's head spun.

"I must say," said the older Wingwot, "it's not common for a hedgehog to live alone."

"What do you mean? Don't all hedgehogs live alone?"

That sent the Wingwots into another titter.

"Don't you know?" said a Wingwot almost in a reprimand. "Most hedgehogs live in a village by the sea."

"In a *village*?"

"And for you never to be preyed upon—well, you've been very fortunate indeed, young fellow. It's a dangerous world out there."

"Maybe you should just go back to your home and stay safe. Let your friend come back when he's ready," suggested a husky Wingwot in a gravelly voice.

How tempting that seemed to Horatio at this moment. If only he knew for sure Rollic would come back. But the sound of the river roared inside him even louder now. "I hear you," Horatio answered silently.

"No," Horatio said to the Wingwots, "I *have* to find him."

"Well, your friend could have been eaten himself—a large water snake would be my bet—and there wouldn't be anything left of him *to find*."

"Please," chided the older Wingwot, "there's no reason to be rude."

"There are predators of otters?" Horatio couldn't believe it.

"Of course, although not as many as there are of hedgehogs."

Horatio gasped.

"Stop," pleaded the older Wingwot. "You're going to frighten him to death."

Horatio tried to keep his composure. "I have this sense Rollic's still alive."

"Then he probably is," the older Wingwot blurted out. "I remember when my wife Meerious disappeared. She simply wanted to smell some sea air. It was about this time last year. I wrote this poem about her when we first met." He stretched out his arms:

"Oh, Meerious, I'm delirious. I'm in love.
What you do to me is mysterious.
Of all the Wingwots, you're imperious.
Oh, Meerious, let's get serious. I'm in love."

The Wingwots applauded quietly with their wings, which made the rock sparkle. "That was beautiful, Winfred," one Wingwot exclaimed.

Horatio found himself applauding too. "But she came back?"

The whole rock fell still.

"No, she hasn't."

"Oh," Horatio's paws dropped to his side. His heart sank. He suddenly felt more alone than ever. Would the sound of the river churning inside him be all he'd have left of Rollic?

"But that doesn't mean I've given up hope." Out of the stillness, Winfred alighted off the rock and hovered above Horatio. Horatio put out his paw and Winfred landed on it. "Just because my wife hasn't come back doesn't mean your friend won't," the old Wingwot told him. "I know how you feel right now. It's a lonely, empty feeling. But if you sense your friend is still alive, don't let anyone tell you otherwise." Horatio nodded. "Go out there and find him." Horatio nodded again. "May I make a suggestion?"

"Please do," thought Horatio.

"If you don't know exactly where your friend went, why don't you head for a place that's safe? The Forest of Epoh is not too far from here. It's a very pleasant forest. No predators to bother you there. From there you can decide where to go next."

That sounded like a sensible idea. Horatio began to feel a bit better. "How would I get there?"

"Follow the river south, until you see a clump of trees and boulders in the middle of the river. At that point, go due east. You'll soon reach the Forest of Epoh."

"Due east," repeated Horatio. "Which way is east?"

"Away from the river."

"Oh, right. Got it." Horatio's ears turned pink.

Winfred fluttered back up to the rock. "I'll tell you what. We'll keep an eye out for your friend. Up in the sky, we can see things you can't see from the ground. Does your otter friend have any traits we could recognize him by?"

"Well, he's all brown, but his two front paws are white."

"White paws. Good, very good. We don't see many otters with white paws."

"Thanks," said Horatio. "To the Forest of Epoh," he declared with all the conviction he could muster. He headed off at a fast gait. "Good-bye," he waved.

"Farewell. Good luck." The Wingwots waved back. Their wings flapped briskly, making the rock come to life in gold.

Chapter 3

Whisklet and Whimser

Horatio followed the riverbank south. With every crunch or rustle of a leaf, he feared some fox or ferret might pounce on him. With every wisp of wind, he would crouch down and lurch his head upward, thinking it might be a hawk.

His whole world seemed to have been turned upside down. He was separated from his best and only friend, separated from a village where his own kind lived, a village he knew nothing about until now, alone in a world where predators roamed all around him.

He wondered why Rollic had never mentioned predators before. "Maybe he didn't want to scare me," he thought. "Or maybe *he* never encountered a predator before in his life."

He was glad the Wingwots would keep an eye out for Rollic. But another question perplexed him. Why did he live alone if other hedgehogs lived in a village by the sea?

"I'm sure if Rollic had known about the hedgehog village, he would have told me."

Horatio saw the fork in the river, with a grove of trees and heavy rocks in the middle. "Those must be the boulders." He turned east toward the Forest of Epoh and climbed up a steep, mossy embankment. In the distance he saw a field of purple, orange, and yellow wildflowers, and farther beyond them a dense forest. He began to run, spurred on by the beauty of the wildflowers and the safe haven of the forest.

Arriving in the middle of the field, his senses took over. He buried his nose in the flowers and inhaled their scent. For a moment his worries seemed to fade a little. The world couldn't be so bad with such wonderful wildflowers. He barely noticed how a cloud seemed to cast a shadow over the flowers where he stood. Only when the cloud grew darker, making Horatio feel there might be a sudden burst of rain, did he look up into a massive hurling shape of wings. When he saw a yellow beak open and red eyes searing down on him, he understood. He was being attacked! His heart exploded inside him. He could hardly breathe. His needles instinctively flared out. He made a run for it, scurrying through the wildflowers. Realizing he couldn't outrun it, he hunkered down into a ball of spikes. His knapsack's straps squeezed tight around

him, and all of a sudden he had the sensation his feet were lifting off the ground. He felt no pain. It seemed as if the hawk's claws had penetrated only his knapsack.

Two loud snaps rang out, and suddenly he was in a free fall straight to the ground. He landed with a thud, rolling over and over. Not losing a second, he scampered as fast as he could toward the forest, ducking behind the nearest tree he could find. He peaked out once to see his knapsack, landing like a lump in the middle of the field. "The straps must have broken." The distant cry of the hawk echoed away in the sky.

He pressed against the tree, his eyes shut tight, his heart pounding so loud it filled his ears. He vaguely heard a voice talking to him, "Hey, little fella. Are you okay?"

"Hey, Whisklet, come here! It's a hedgehog!"

"Right, a hedgehog. You think I would fall for that?"

"No, really! A hawk almost got it. Come here, quick!"

Horatio opened his eyes to see a figure of a hamster in front of him. Then another hamster appeared. The first wore a red bandana and the second a blue one; other than that they looked almost identical. They had on broad-brimmed hats, plaid shirts, and blue jeans full of patches. They each held a staff, slightly taller than they were.

"Are you okay? How did you get here?" asked the hamster with the red bandana.

He closed his eyes and opened them again. The hamsters were still there. He wasn't imagining them.

The first hamster's voice became more reassuring, "You're safe now. You're not hurt, are you?"

Horatio calmed his breathing. "I think I'm okay." He tested one leg, then the other, then his two front paws. He looked all over himself—no blood. "I'm not bleeding am I?"

"No, not that we can see. You're awfully lucky," said the second hamster.

"He came so suddenly. I had no idea he was there." Horatio held himself tight against the tree, as if he would plummet if he let go.

"You're safe here. You're in the Forest of Epoh. I'm Whisklet," Whisklet took off his hat. He felt like patting Horatio on the back to reassure him, but with the spikes all over him, he wasn't sure how to do that. Instead, he extended his arm to shake paws.

"Nice to meet you," Horatio shook Whisklet's paw. "My name's Horatio."

"I'm Whimser." The other hamster took his hat off too, and grasped Horatio's paw very gently fearing it might be sore. "What brings you here?"

Horatio told them about his search for Rollic and how the Wingwots had advised him to come here.

"How have you made it this far? There aren't any hedgehogs who live near here."

"I live up north along the river. Not too far away."

"Is there a hedgehog community there?"

"No, I live by myself."

"Really?" asked Whisklet. "Who raised you?"

"I don't remember anyone raising me. I thought all hedgehogs lived alone. At least I did until I met the Wingwots. They told me about a hedgehog village." Horatio shrugged. "I didn't even know there was a hedgehog village."

"They're right. There is a village along the sea. Are you a Solety?" asked Whimser.

"What's a Solety?"

Whimser took off his hat again and scratched his head. He couldn't quite figure out this little animal in front of him. "You've never heard of a Solety before?"

"No."

"Well," Whimser lifted his chin and scratched his neck, trying to think how to explain it. "It's really not that uncommon for small mammals. Not that uncommon at all. You see, sometimes, a small mammal will lose his parents at a young age. Even before he's fully ready to fend for himself. His parents might have been killed by a predator, or perhaps they couldn't find enough food in the winter. Then he'd have to raise himself. That's a Solety."

Horatio didn't like the idea that he had survived some kind of misfortune. It hadn't occurred to him that his parents might have been killed. He had simply presumed all hedgehogs lived alone. "To think, I could be living with my family right now, as other hedgehogs do," he said to himself.

Then a thought dawned on Horatio. "But how did I end up in a burrow so far away? Why wouldn't I still be with my village? Unless my parents left the village for some reason."

That had both Whisklet and Whimser stumped. Whimser came up with an answer, "Maybe your parents were pioneers. Setting out for a better life. They were pioneers and you're," Whimser punched the air with his paw, "*a survivor!*"

Horatio could tell Whimser was trying to make him feel better. But it wasn't working very well. "Do you two have parents?"

Whisklet nodded, "They live in a burrow not too far from here, on the other side of the forest. We're old enough to live in our own burrow now."

Hearing the hamsters had parents only made Horatio feel worse, and he was a bit ashamed of himself for feeling that way.

"You shouldn't feel bad about being a Solety," said Whisklet. "There isn't a small mammal anywhere who couldn't see himself in your paws. All of us know we could have found ourselves on our own, without someone to look after us."

Neither Whisklet nor Whimser knew what more to say. The little hedgehog sitting at the base of the tree intrigued them. They had never seen a real hedgehog before, only read about them in a book.

"I tell you what," said Whisklet, "small mammals like us need to stick together. Look, we haven't gone on an adventure for a while. Why don't we accompany you?"

"How about it!" Whimser nodded. "It isn't safe to travel alone, and we've got a lot of experience staying away from predators."

Horatio's face beamed. He was almost speechless. "Do you really mean it?"

"Of course."

"That would be wonderful!"

Horatio's broad smile heartened the hamsters. "That settles it, then. So tell me," said Whisklet, "where do you think your otter friend went?"

"He was going to visit a swimming hole. A popular one." Horatio didn't want to tell them about the sound of the river inside him, the sound of Rollic calling to him. He wasn't sure they'd understand.

"We know just about every swimming hole on this side of the river. There's one with a waterfall slide otters love. We can take you to it."

"That would be ..." Horatio was at a loss for words. "Wonderful!" he repeated.

"How were you planning on getting there?" asked Whisklet.

"Well, the Wingwots told me to come here to the Forest of Epoh, and I was planning to head that way," Horatio pointed his paw straight ahead of him.

Whisklet looked around him. They were in the middle of a forest. There was no path to follow. "You were just going to go that way?" He raised his paw in the direction Horatio had.

"Uh-huh," Horatio nodded.

"And walk into a swimming hole."

"Not much of a plan?"

"Honk!" Whimser broke out laughing. "Honk!"

Horatio had never heard a honk come out of a mammal. His shock made Whisklet burst into laughter. "The look on your face," he pointed to Horatio. "I know. I know. No one laughs like my brother," he slapped Whimser on the back.

"Honk! Honk!" Whimser couldn't stop. This was just too much for Horatio and he started laughing out loud.

"Oh, my," said Whisklet, wiping his eyes, as he tried to compose himself. "It's not going to be that easy to get to the swimming holes. It's several days' travel. Did you bring anything with you for the trip?"

"I brought a knapsack full of food. But the hawk dropped it in the middle of the field. I don't want to go back there."

"No, you shouldn't. That's outside the Forest of Epoh. It's prime hunting ground for hawks."

"We can get it for you," a high-pitched voice called out.

Horatio spotted two small chubby snails gliding slowly down the tree toward him. "I didn't know snails could talk," said Horatio.

"These aren't your usual snails," said Whimser. "They can talk to insects, mammals, reptiles, amphibians, birds. They speak more languages than anyone I know."

"Well, we ushually don't like to talk to birdsh. Or anything elshe that might eat ush. I'm Mish, and thish ish my brother Mosh," said Mish.

"Nishe to meet you," said Mosh.

"Nishe, I mean nice to meet you," said Horatio.

"We'll bring your knapshack right back," said Mish.

Horatio waited, but the snails didn't seem to be going anywhere. If they were moving, they were progressing at the most sluggish pace (a term Mish and Mosh would have found particularly offensive). Horatio couldn't imagine how two small snails could manage to push his knapsack all the way from the field.

Whimser seemed to read Horatio's mind. "I know what you're thinking. You're thinking it would take snails forever to get your knapsack back, right?"

Horatio nodded ever so slightly, trying hard not to offend anyone.

"Well, when you watch them, it does look like they're hardly moving. But when you don't watch them, it's amazing how much ground they cover. Tell me, have you ever seen how fast snails move when you're *not* watching them?"

Horatio thought about it a while. "No, I guess I haven't."

"Well, neither has anyone else. I think it's a common misconception that snails move slowly. They just don't like to be watched. How would you feel if everyone watched you to see how fast you moved?"

"I'm not sure," said Horatio.

"Well, I don't think you'd like it. Mish and Mosh can move like lightening—when no one is watching. Just leave it to them. If they say they can get your knapsack back, they probably can. They've helped us in our travels more than we can say." He waved his paw in the direction of the snails. When Horatio glanced at them, they still didn't seem to be moving.

"Let's think about what we'll need for the trip," said Whisklet. "We'll need rope, pocketknives, and flint to make a fire."

"And another one of these hats," said Whimser. He took the hat off his head. "We have an extra one you can wear. It comes in real handy. If you wear it with the brim all the way out it makes you look bigger from above, which is always a good thing. You can roll it up," Whimser showed him how, "and use it as a pillow at night." He tucked it between his shoulder and the side of his face. "You can swat away bugs with it." He unrolled it fully and gave a short swatting demonstration. "If you shake it like this, you can use it to stoke the campfire. Or hold it in front of your face to keep the smoke away. I could go on and on about these hats. We'll lend you one." He put his own hat back on.

"Thanks," said Horatio, taken aback. He couldn't recall anyone ever lending him anything.

"We'll need a good map," said Whisklet. "We should talk to Graysent. He has the most detailed maps of the region."

Whimser cocked his head proudly, "Would you like to meet him?"

"Graysent?" Horatio asked.

Whimser's chest deflated. "You haven't heard of him?"

Horatio shook his head, hoping once again not to have offended anyone.

"You really have lived on your own, haven't you?

Graysent's a great gray owl and the protector of the Forest of Epoh. He's issued an edict that prohibits predators from hunting in this forest. That's why you're safe here. He's a hero to small mammals like us."

Horatio felt an immediate reverence for the owl, knowing all too well now what it meant for a small mammal to be safe from predators. "You two know him?"

Whimser beamed, "We sure do. He's been a friend of our family's, going back to when our grandfather was a boy."

"Wow," Horatio was duly impressed.

"Hey, look!" Whimser pointed toward the field.

Horatio turned. There, in the middle of the field, sat Mish and Mosh atop his knapsack. His mouth fell open. "How did they get there so fast?"

"Ha!" Whimser laughed, "I told you. They aren't your usual snails."

Mish and Mosh couldn't give a thumbs-up sign, but they had fully extended themselves out of their shells, as if to signal "everything's under control." Then they both disappeared inside the knapsack and didn't come out.

"I tell you what," said Whisklet, "while they're bringing your knapsack back, why don't we visit Graysent about the map. Are you ready?"

Horatio stood up. His legs felt fine. He wasn't the least bit wobbly. "Ready!" he said.

"Good. This should be a grand trip."

Chapter 4

Graysent

The three small mammals entered a forest of ancient trees with gnarled trunks. Enormous ferns blanketed the forest floor. An old majestic tree, whose trunk was so gnarled and twisted, it looked like it was wrestling with itself, stood in a small clearing. The other trees seemed to be keeping their distance out of deference. About two-thirds of the way up the tree appeared a neat oval opening.

Whisklet called up, "Graysent, it's Whisklet. Could we have a moment of your time?"

There was no response for quite a while, but Whisklet didn't call twice. Then out of the hole appeared a large great gray owl, with penetrating yellow eyes, set deep into his face. Numerous rings encircled his eyes, making him look exceedingly weary, as if he had seen many things in his long life—and many things he wished he hadn't.

"Whisklet, Whimser, good day to you." His voice

seemed surprisingly gentle to Horatio for such an imposing creature. He climbed out of the hole and rested on the branch next to it.

Whisklet began, "We found a hedgehog. His name's Horatio. A hawk tried to grab him. He escaped though. Wasn't hurt. He's looking for his otter friend. We were hoping to borrow a map so we could take him to some swimming holes where the otter might have gone."

Graysent bent over to get a good look at Horatio from the branch.

"You seem to be far from home, Horatio."

"I live by myself north of here, along the riverbank." Horatio now realized he would need to explain where he lived to just about everyone he met. Graysent looked down at him quizzically.

"We think Horatio's a Solety," said Whimser. Horatio's ears turned pink.

"I see. But you're not sure?" Horatio shook his head. "Ahh, so you've been on your own a long time?" Horatio nodded. "And now you've set off to find your friend?" Horatio nodded again. "What's your friend's name?"

"Rollic."

"And what makes you think Rollic won't return on his own accord?"

"It's been days now. It's not like him to stay away from home this long. And I have a sense he needs my help."

"What do you mean 'a sense'? What kind of sense?"

Horatio looked back and forth at the hamsters, then

took a deep breath before he spoke. "I have a sense he's calling me." His ears turned pink again.

"You hear his voice?"

"No, not his voice." He wasn't sure how to explain it. "I hear the sound of the river rushing inside of me. Something tells me the sound's Rollic. He's calling to me." Horatio suspected they would think this was all silliness, but when he looked at Graysent, the owl's face had turned grave.

"Do you *ever* hear his voice?" asked Graysent.

"No, never his voice."

"A sound that *reminds* you of Rollic?"

"It's more than that. I know it's Rollic."

"It's a sound that is the essence of Rollic. What Rollic would be if he ever became purely a sound?"

"Yes, that's it." Graysent seemed to understand perfectly.

Graysent lifted his wing, "Let me get you a map." He disappeared back into his hole. A few moments later, Graysent reappeared, holding a rolled up scroll, clutched in his right claw. The huge bird alighted from the hole, and set down on the ground so softly next to the three small mammals that Horatio, even with the hawk attack fresh in his mind, did not flinch.

Graysent inhaled deeply. He gestured with his wing, "Before I show you the map, I need to tell you a tale so you know what you might be getting yourselves into. Please, have a seat." The animals sat down on the floor of the forest, amid dry leaves from seasons past.

"Near the point where the river meets the sea, there's a beach full of beautiful stones. They say a few of the stones have magical powers. They will grant you a wish. But not every creature can make the magical powers emerge from a stone—the stone must be right for the one who holds it.

"A creature, who calls himself Scarretchen, guards these stones. He punishes anyone who trespasses. He has the power to change himself or any other animal into any type of creature he chooses. He may transform an innocent squirrel, scurrying by, into a worm. The creature will retain the mind of a squirrel but be in the body of a worm. Then Scarretchen will keep the worm inside a glass jar along with other creatures he has trapped.

"He will make a game out of it. He will give the entrapped animal the power to call to a friend or loved one to come to its rescue. For the only way a creature can be turned back to its original form is if the friend or loved one recognizes it and says its name out loud.

"Unable to resist the calls for help, they come to their loved one's rescue, come to the beach full of stones—only to become another of Scarretchen's victims. He must have trapped scores of animals in his lair—brothers, sisters, parents and their children, best friends.

"I do not know for sure if the sound you hear is your friend calling you for help. But there are telltale signs. You hear only his essence, not his voice. For hearing the essence of someone is even more powerful than hearing his voice. Scarretchen's victims communicate to their friends without words, only with sounds—the sounds of their truest selves. For this reason, you feel so clearly they are with you."

"Yes," said Horatio. "That's how it is."

The three small mammals sat there stunned. Just a few minutes ago they had thought they would be off on an adventure to find a wayward otter.

"What kind of creature is Scarretchen?" asked Whisklet.

"I don't know if anyone knows for sure. He's a creature of his own design. He was a man." The small mammals' mouths fell open. "That's right, a human—one of the few who have ever visited this part of the world. He lived happily in a large castle, until his wife died carrying his unborn child. So grief stricken by his wife's death, and the loss of his child, he locked himself into his library of books. One day he found an ancient book in a dusty, hidden compartment within one of the shelves of his library. The book contained a map, which showed the destination of the wishing stones. He traveled by ship across the seas to get to these stones.

"The first wish he made was to bring his wife back to life. When he returned to his castle, she was not there. He presumed the wishing stone had not worked. That it was just a myth. But later that night, through the cold windy rain, he heard a small meow outside. When he opened the front door of his castle, there stood a tabby cat. And in the faint light, he could tell by the sound of her meow that this was his wife. She had been brought back to life, yes—but as a cat. The cat recognized him too as the husband she once had. He was grateful for the company of his wife as a cat. But he wanted her back for real, and he wanted his child-to-be back as well.

"So he crossed the seas a second time. He returned to the wishing stones and made another wish. This time he wished his wife would return in human form as she was before she died. When he got back to his castle, there stood his wife as a woman, no longer as a cat. But his wife did not recognize him. You see, the wishing stones have an unusual quality—whenever they grant you a wish they take something away from you. In his first wish, his wife came back to life but not as a human. In the second wish, she came back as a human but did not know who he was. She demanded that the butler throw him out. Without his wife and now without his home, he returned across the seas to the wishing stones a third time.

"This time he wished for his wife to know and love him." Graysent stopped and sighed. He lifted his wings, "A wish anyone might ask for, but this wish turned out to be the worst of all. In an instant, he had turned into a cockatoo and found himself in a cage in his castle. His wife, still in human form, cooed at him lovingly. She knew and loved him as a pet. She did not know that inside the bird lived the man who had been her husband. She loved the bird so much, she would not let him out of his cage—she did not want him to escape. So he couldn't return to the wishing stones to make another wish. A month later, his wife gave birth to his son. Then she learned her husband's ship sank on the return trip. She thought her husband was lost at sea. Eventually, she fell in love and married another man, who lived in the castle together with her and Scarretchen's son.

"There Scarretchen sat, day after day, a man inside the body of a caged bird, watching another man take Scarretchen's place in his wife's heart, another man become the father to Scarretchen's son. His wife—the woman who used to be his wife that is—cooed at him lovingly through the bars of his cage. He felt like she was taunting him. 'Did she really not know who he was?' he began to wonder. His love for her fell away from him like molting feathers. He had to break free, but there was no escape. He forgot what it was like to be human. He started to hate all humans for the cruel ways they enslaved animals. But he never accepted himself as an animal, either. He held animals in contempt, thinking them weak and powerless. He grew to hate all creatures.

"Then one day, his boy, who was about three years old, opened his cage by accident. Scarretchen broke loose and flew out through an open window. He flew back across the seas to the wishing stones. He made another wish—to have the power to turn himself, or any creature, into any living thing he chose. He would avenge his years as a caged bird by inflicting cruelty upon others. And then he turned himself into the half-man, half-beast that he is today—the most dangerous of all creatures.

"I've told you this so you know what you're facing. If it is Scarretchen who has captured your friend, you need to decide for yourselves if you wish to continue on."

Horatio felt everyone's eyes on him. He wasn't sure if he would have the courage to rescue Rollic. He picked up some dry leaves and crumpled them in his paws, watching the bits fall to the ground. At last he spoke. "How could I live with myself if I knew Rollic was out there, needing my help, calling for *me*, and yet I did nothing about it? How could I just go about my days as if nothing had happened?" It felt like a huge lump was welling up in his throat. He had no desire to be another of Scarretchen's victims. His throat was so tight, it hurt to speak, the lump seemed to press on him. "I may not know much about the world. But I do know Rollic's my friend."

The hamsters stared at Horatio. They saw a strength behind his words that belied his small size. They too knew what loyalty meant.

Whisklet jumped resolutely to his feet. "We said before that small mammals must stick together." He stomped his staff hard into the ground. "Friends of Graysent stand against injustice wherever we see it. Scarretchen shouldn't be allowed to get away with this."

Whimser stood up now. "That's right." The staff trembled in his paw. He needed both paws to hold it still. "Besides, we know a thing or two about staying ahead of trouble. Don't we?" He tapped his staff on the ground.

"Against injustice."

Now Horatio stood up. "Against injustice."

Graysent's sad eyes glowed with pride, but revealed no hint of surprise. "Let me show you the map."

Graysent unfurled the map—a beautifully detailed drawing unlike anything Horatio had seen. Horatio could easily identify the river. For the first time he could see how it curved like a twisting snake. He realized now how big a world he lived in. "I could travel all my life and not see everything," he thought.

"Here is where the river reaches the sea," Graysent pointed with his wing. "To the east, lies the hedgehog village. To the west, in this small inlet, lie the wishing stones. Just north of where the river meets the sea lies the Great Blue Bog. A friend of mine lives there. His name is Francis Hopper. He's the only creature known to have come face-to-face with Scarretchen and lived to tell about it. He's an old bullfrog now and a wise and trusted friend. You should visit with him. He may be able to give you some advice. You'll need to cross the river to reach him."

"How in the world could they cross the river?" Horatio wondered, but the hamsters didn't seem concerned.

"Your small size may actually serve to your advantage. You may be able to sneak up on Scarretchen's lair without him noticing."

"Thank you," said Whisklet as Graysent rolled the map back up into his claw and handed it to him. "We'll bring it back."

"Simply bring yourselves back—with or without the map," Graysent sighed deeply. The weariness Horatio had first seen in his face seemed more pronounced now.

"To your safe return," Graysent held his wing out. Whisklet and Whimser placed their paws on it. Horatio did the same.

"To a safe return," they all said.

Graysent flew back up to his home in the tree. He turned to give them one last look and then vanished into his hole.

Chapter 5

The Feat and Feast of Mish and Mosh

When the three small mammals returned to the tree where they first met, Mish and Mosh were waiting for them with Horatio's knapsack.

"You did it!" Horatio exclaimed. The sentiment he had for his knapsack began to flood over him.

"What did I say? They're not your usual snails!" said Whimser.

Horatio would have given his knapsack a great big hug if there had been no one else around to see. He started to pick it up then dropped it. "It's covered in slime!"

"We had to shlime it real good, to get it to move," said Mish.

"Don't worry," Whimser cut in quickly, "that can be washed off."

Horatio lifted it into the air with his arms outstretched to keep the slime away from his fur. The knapsack seemed much lighter now. Then he noticed the snails' faces were a lot plumper than he had remembered. He peered inside his knapsack. "My food is gone!"

"Mish and Mosh!" cried Whimser. "That wasn't your food to eat."

"Well, we had to do *shomething* to lighten the load," said Mish.

"To make it eashier to push," said Mosh. "And it got eashier and eashier, the more we ate."

"Beshides," said Mish, "where the hawk'sh clawsh put holesh in the knapshack, he alsho shquished a lot of the berriesh, made a terrible mesh inshide." Horatio could see the puncture holes from the hawk's claws. "We ate it up ... I mean cleaned it up, the besht we could."

"I didn't know snails could eat a whole supply of food," said Horatio. He didn't want to sound ungrateful. "At least you were able to get my knapsack back."

"Don't worry about the food, Horatio," Whisklet offered. "We have plenty of food in our burrow, enough for all of us."

"Thanks," said Horatio. "I appreciate it."

"Let's go back to our burrow and pack for the trip."

Horatio stopped. "That's odd. I thought the straps of my knapsack had broken. I thought that's why I fell.

I thought I heard them snap. But the straps are perfectly fine."

"He must have lost his grip on you," said Whisklet.

"Maybe it was my spikes. Maybe they pricked him and made him let me go."

"No, he wouldn't have even felt your spikes. His claws are as tough as a rock."

"Maybe you wiggled loose from your knapsack," said Whimser.

"I don't remember wiggling."

Mish and Mosh sat there bemused, as the three small mammals studied the straps on Horatio's knapsack. The snails hadn't gotten into nearly as much trouble as they thought they would for eating Horatio's food.

"Who knows why he dropped you?" said Whisklet. "Some things you have to put down as luck."

"Other than a couple of holes in it, my knapsack is fine."

"Just a bit slimy, that's all," Whimser said. "We'll wash that off. Let's get some chow."

The group headed to the hamsters' home. Horatio held his knapsack out away from him.

"You two already ate dinner, didn't you?" Whisklet asked the snails.

"Well," Mish eyed Mosh, "I think we might have left room for desshert."

"I can't wait to show you my snake charmer, Horatio," Whimser said.

"A snake charmer?"

"It hypnotizes snakes when I play it. Come on, I'll show you how it works."

As they tramped through the forest, a question popped into Horatio's mind. "Whimser? If I'm the first hedgehog you've seen, how did you even know I was a hedgehog?"

"We've read about hedgehogs and seen pictures of them in books."

"Books, right. I have a vague memory of seeing a book once."

Whimser laughed with a honk. "You really have been on your own."

Chapter 6

Packing Up

For Horatio, whose only possessions were his knapsack and the clothes he wore, Whisklet and Whimser's burrow seemed to be overflowing with their belongings. There were musical instruments, books, artwork made from all sorts of woodland materials—bark, flowers, and leaves—and something Horatio had never seen, a fireplace inside the burrow for cooking.

Whimser washed the slime off of Horatio's knapsack in a bucket of water, while Whisklet got a fire going, and heated up a hazelnut plum casserole for their dinner.

Whimser could tell by the embroidery on Horatio's knapsack—the curly red letters of Horatio's name encircled by stars—that it was made when Horatio was little. He knew most small mammals Horatio's age would have outgrown this knapsack, and would have asked their parents for a new one. But, of course, Horatio had no parents he could ask. Whimser hung Horatio's knapsack safely over the fire to dry.

"Now here's my snake charmer I was telling you about. I would never travel without it."

"Where did you get it?"

"From a journey rat. He traded it to me for a blueberry pie. It's amazing what rats will do for some good food. Of course, when I traded with him, I didn't know for sure if it would work. But now that I do, it's the best trade I ever made."

"Really? Let's hear it."

Whimser started to play an eerie, mesmerizing tune. Horatio could almost feel his body sway involuntarily to the music. Whimser stopped. "Fortunately, it doesn't hypnotize mammals." Horatio was still swaying a bit. "Right, Horatio?" Whimser winked.

"Right," Horatio answered, bringing himself back.

"It seems to work only on snakes. And it doesn't seem to matter what size snake; the music gets to them all in the same way, as far as I can tell."

"So you've actually tried it on snakes before?"

"Several times."

"What was it like the first time you tried it on a snake—how did you know it would work?"

"We didn't—but we had a backup plan."

"What was that?"

"RUN!" Whimser honked. They all started laughing.

"Here's the extra hat I mentioned to you," said Whimser. "You can hold nuts and berries in it, scoop it into the river to get a drink, carry sticks for the fire with it." He was about to recite a new list of things to do with the hat, but stopped himself. He tossed the hat to Horatio.

"Thanks!" Horatio put it on. It fit him well.

"We'll each take a pocketknife," said Whimser, handing one to Horatio. "Have you ever used one?"

"No," said Horatio. He hadn't even seen one before, but didn't want to say so.

"Here's how you take the blade out. You'll want to be careful with it."

"Here's the flint for making fires," said Whisklet. "We'll need rope too. It comes in handy in emergencies. We'll put the rope in your knapsack, Horatio. We'll put the food in mine. We've got sacks of blackberries, blueberries, mushrooms," he said, holding each one up. "Hazelnuts, dandelions, and pinecone seeds."

"We'll also need canteens for drinking water," said Whimser. "Especially if we get away from the river."

"Let's take a look at the map," said Whisklet. He found a spot on the floor far enough away from the fire to unroll it. "Here's where we are." He pointed to a forested area of the map marked Epoh. "We could cut through the forest and travel along the river, but it curves so much—that would be the long way to go. Or we can travel to the end of the Forest of Epoh and take the shorter route through Glob Swamp."

Whimser gave an audible gulp.

"What's in Glob Swamp?" asked Horatio.

"Quicksand," said Whisklet. "I'm told it looks like mud, but if you step in it, it will suck you down before you even have time to yelp. We've never been there before. Usually we'd go along the river. But that could take several more days of travel."

"I don't know if Rollic has that long," said Horatio softly.

"We know mud," said Mish. "We can tell the difference between quickshand and mud."

"Can you really?" asked Whisklet.

"Shure," said Mosh. "We're expertsh."

"Through Glob Swamp then?" Whisklet asked the group. Whimser and Horatio nodded. "We'll only travel through it during the day, and we'll make sure to keep to dry land." Whisklet pointed to a spot on the map farther south. "Now here are good swimming holes." His claw pointed to small spots of blue on the map. "This is the one with the waterfall slide otters love. We've been there. I think we should check it out. That's the one Rollic probably had in mind. The more we know about what happened to Rollic, the better prepared we'll be."

"What's this mean?" Horatio pointed to some rolling lines on the map that crossed the river. It was south of Glob Swamp and north of the swimming holes.

"That's the waterfall," said Whimser. "A huge waterfall."

"Rollic told me about that. He said the current took

him right over the waterfall."

"Even for a river otter that's dangerous."

"What's the bow and arrow on the map?" asked Horatio. He pointed to a spot near the swimming holes.

"How do you know what a bow and arrow is?" asked Whisklet.

"I just do. I don't know how. There's an arrow through one of the stars on my knapsack."

"Have you ever shot one?"

"No."

"That's where they hold the Tournament of Archers each year, in the summer," said Whimser. "They should be having this year's tournament in a couple of days. We might be able to watch some of it. It's in the same direction we need to go. I know we don't have time to spare, but hedgehogs are legendary for their archery skills."

"You're kidding me," said Horatio, his ears turning pink.

"No, really. The champion from the hedgehog village will be there. You might even be able to meet him."

"I've never met another hedgehog before."

"Who knows?" said Whisklet. "He might even be able to tell you more about where you came from and how you ended up by yourself."

"I *would* like to know." A sense of excitement rose up in Horatio.

"Then we'll try to find out." Whisklet said.

They sat quietly in front of the fire, as Whisklet served the casserole in bowls.

"What are your parents like?" Horatio asked them.

"Oh, they're fairly regular folks. My dad's got a bit of a belly, and he's losing some of his fur." Whimser gave a light honk. "I think I got my dad's sense of humor."

"Our dad liked adventure, when he was younger. I think I got that from him," said Whisklet. "I don't like to stay in one place for very long. And our mom was the kindest mother a hamster could want growing up. She has a wonderful singing voice. I think Whimser got his musical ability from her." Whimser nodded.

Horatio couldn't think of any special traits he might have inherited from his parents.

"We're going to go see our parents tomorrow," said Whimser. "So you'll get a chance to meet them. We always stop by before we leave the Forest of Epoh. It's more dangerous out there, outside the Forest."

Horatio listened to the sound of the river droning on inside him. He had the sense Rollic knew he could hear him, perhaps even knew he was on his way, coming to rescue him.

"Horatio," Whisklet said softly, "when we see our parents tomorrow, don't tell them anything about Scarretchen. I don't want them to worry. We'll just say we're going to the Tournament of Archers."

"All right," Horatio nodded.

They stared into the embers of the fire, each reflecting

on his own fears. With the dangers Horatio knew loomed ahead, he let the quiet safety of the burrow, the warmth of the fire, and the fellowship of Whisklet and Whimser sink in, and he understood—deep within him—that this moment would be one he would always remember.

Chapter 7

Venturing Out

The three small mammals headed out first thing that morning. The dew still dampened the ground. The chorus of songbirds still rang out across the forest. Mish and Mosh rode atop Whimser's knapsack.

The day was clear and cool, perfect for a trek through the woods. Horatio walked between the two hamsters. He told himself not to fall behind, not to slip up or trip, not to do anything foolish, or anything that might make his companions reconsider their decision to accompany him.

Unlike the simple walking staffs Whisklet and Whimser held the day before, they now carried aloft ornately designed staffs. The staffs were slightly taller than the

hamsters themselves. Within each staff were carved branches and leaves and woodland creatures— hamsters, moles, squirrels, chipmunks—and on the top of the staff sat the carved face of a great gray owl. Only the eyes of the owl were painted—a bright yellow.

"Those are handsome staffs," said Horatio.

"These are no mere staffs," replied Whisklet. "These are the Emblems of Graysent. We carry these whenever we travel outside the Forest of Epoh. They tell all creatures we're friends of Graysent and are under his protection. No bird of prey, or mammal, would attack a creature carrying the Emblems of Graysent. Even if they have never seen the Emblems before, they will recognize them by the yellow eyes. The yellow eyes are legendary. No other emblem has them."

"What would Graysent do, if they did attack you?"

"It's not so much what he would do, as who he is. He's so highly respected among animals. Even among birds who don't like him so much, like hawks—they still respect him. And if a hawk or some other bird of prey sees we're carrying these Emblems, it will leave us alone."

"Snakes don't understand the Emblems," added Whimser. "That's why we have the snake charmer."

"How did Graysent get to be so respected?"

"It all started with our grandfather," said Whisklet. "Graysent knew our grandfather when they both were young. When they first met, Graysent was still a predator, and he had swooped down on our grandfather to eat him. Our grandfather impressed upon Graysent that he would be eating not just one hamster, but generations and generations of hamsters yet to come, each with the ability to change the world in some way. Graysent was so moved, they became good friends. Graysent swore never to eat another creature again for the rest of his life. That's a remarkable thing for a bird of prey to do—to change his whole way of life. Other owls, over time, came to respect him for his decision. Soon, the other owls in the Forest of Epoh followed his way. Graysent grew to be the patriarch of the owls, and he issued an edict that no predator could come into the Forest of Epoh. Which is why, as long as we are here in this forest, we can walk around without fear. He's truly a hero to small mammals everywhere."

"I think," said Whimser, "seeing us reminds him of the conversation he had with our grandfather all those years ago. We're the generations of hamsters our grandfather spoke about."

Whisklet continued, "When Graysent became the protector of this forest, he told our grandfather to carve this emblem, so whoever saw him carrying it would know not to harm him. My grandfather and the animals of the forest worked long and hard in making this staff. They each carved an image of themselves on it. Then, when my father came of age, they made a second one. You can tell the one I'm holding is older. It was my grandfather's. Both emblems were passed down to us a year ago."

Whisklet stopped and held the staff reverently in both paws in front of Horatio. Horatio could see the contours of the fur on the animals carved into the staff, the points of their claws, their lifelike eyes.

"It must be an honor to be entrusted with them," said Horatio.

"Oh, it is," said Whisklet. It was an honor beyond words.

They started up again. The ferns that covered the ground near their burrow gradually disappeared, and in their place emerged a dense undergrowth of seedlings, mostly small pine trees.

"How old are you two?" Horatio asked.

"We're fifteen," said Whimser. "Whisklet is about ten minutes older than I am."

"How long have you been living in your own burrow?"

"For about two years now. Most hamsters live on their own at about that age. How old are you?"

"I'm not sure. But I've been living by myself in my burrow for seven years. I've counted the seasons."

"I'd say you're about eleven then. Because hedgehogs and hamsters become full grown and can start foraging for themselves when they're about four years old. If you were much older than four when you were left on your own, you'd have more of a memory of who raised you."

"Eleven sounds about right. And I must have been full grown because I've never outgrown my clothes."

"You've worn the same clothes all these years?" Whimser asked. Horatio hadn't realized that was unusual. "They must be well made."

They hiked all morning, and the sun had already passed high noon, when they reached a section of the forest full of berry bushes. Two hamsters in the distance were foraging, filling their sacks.

Whisklet and Whimser started to run ahead at a fast gait, and suddenly all four hamsters were in a warm embrace. It was then that Horatio realized that these were their parents.

Whisklet and Whimser grinned sheepishly in their parents' presence as Horatio reached the group. For the first time Horatio saw them as youngsters like himself. Horatio had imagined the parents would be more imposing—"like the river." But they were squat with grayish fur, and Whisklet and Whimser loomed over them.

"My goodness!" the hamsters' father exclaimed at seeing Horatio. "A hedgehog in these woods!"

"This is Horatio," Whimser introduced him.

"What brings a hedgehog so far from home?"

"I live upriver north of here."

"Are there hedgehogs there? I didn't know that."

Horatio smiled awkwardly at having to answer these questions once more. Whimser answered for him. "He's a Solety."

"Ahh," their parents mouthed silently. The hamsters' mother looked at him sympathetically.

Horatio stared at his feet as if they were sinking into the ground.

"Where are you boys off to?" their father asked.

"We're taking Horatio to the Tournament of Archers."

"Are you competing in it?"

"Me? Oh, no. I'm just going to watch."

"The Tournament of Archers," their father sighed wistfully, "that should be exciting."

"It's a long trip. Did you bring enough to eat?" the hamsters' mother asked.

"We did."

"Do you have enough water?"

"We do."

"Horatio isn't wearing a bandana. I really think he should have one. How else will he keep his face and paws clean?" The hamsters and Horatio could think of no response. "I'll get an extra bandana for Horatio."

She darted inside their burrow and came out carrying a green bandana and some things she had baked. "This is a bandana you boys used to wear when you were younger. I picked a green one so everyone will know whose bandana is whose." She put it around Horatio's neck, which made Horatio blush. "Now, Whisklet's is blue, Whimser's red, and Horatio's green," she said with satisfaction. Although she wasn't his mother, Horatio felt comforted knowing someone cared about him enough to tie a bandana around his neck.

"Thank you," said Horatio.

"Here's a pecan tart I made yesterday. And some of my biscuits you love. You boys take them with you."

"Thank you," they each said in turn. Whisklet spied the hungry eyes of Mish and Mosh atop Whimser's knapsack. He put the biscuits inside his own knapsack and the tart inside Horatio's.

"Take good care," their father said.

Their mother held both of their paws for a long moment. "Stay safe," she stared intently at them.

"We will."

The traveling companions set off. When they were out of sight of the hamsters' parents, Horatio asked Whisklet, "Do you think we should have told them about Rollic? Maybe they saw an otter come through the woods the other day."

"No, I didn't want to have to explain why he went missing or say anything that might stir up more questions."

They arrived at the end of the Forest of Epoh, and looked out upon a field of golden grass that radiated in the sun, now hanging low in the sky. They all knew the dangers of an open field. Birds of prey could see the movement of grass from above. Snakes could hide and attack by surprise.

"We have to get across this field before dusk," said

Whisklet. "That's when predators are most on the prowl. I don't want to wait until the morning either. They're hungry in the morning too.

"Once we leave the Forest of Epoh, we're on our own. Even when we're carrying the Emblems anything could happen,"Whisklet explained to Horatio. "You ready?"

Horatio's memory of the hawk attack came flashing back. "Ready," Horatio nodded.

They entered the field. Whisklet and Whimser held the Emblems high. Although the grass rose well above their heads, it was soft and airy, so it bent easily as the small mammals pushed it back with their paws. At times the grass rose higher than the Emblems themselves. Mish and Mosh scanned the sky for any sign of trouble, from atop Whimser's knapsack.

Whisklet led the group onward, keeping a keen eye for matted down grass or any noticeable trail from some other animal.

Whimser heard a blade of grass snap behind them and a faint slithering sound. "Freeze," he motioned to Horatio. Mish and Mosh immediately dropped from the knapsacks to the ground. Horatio could tell this was a drill the hamsters and snails knew well.

Whimser took out his snake charmer and handed the Emblem to Horatio. Mish and Mosh were nowhere to be seen.

Moments later they heard two loud whistles. "They've found the snake. It's got our scent,"Whisklet whispered.

Whimser started to play the snake charmer, the same mesmerizing melody Horatio had heard in their burrow. Whisklet motioned to Horatio, and they began to back up slowly—readying their staffs to strike the second a snake's head popped through the grass.

Then they heard three loud whistles. Whisklet lowered his staff and smiled at Horatio. "It worked. The snake's been hypnotized. Let's go." With Whimser playing on the move, they hurried out of the field.

Once through the field, they waited for Mish and Mosh. Whimser continued playing, so the snails would be able to find them. In no time at all, Horatio saw the snails appear. But it seemed once again as if they were hardly moving. Horatio knew better now. He closed his eyes, waited a few seconds, and reopened them to find Mish and Mosh back atop Whimser's knapsack.

"I didn't know snails could whistle," Horatio said, patting them on their shells to congratulate them.

Whimser grinned proudly. "Their whistle is at such a high pitch that birds, reptiles, amphibians, and even larger mammals can't hear it. Only small mammals like us can. That way they can warn us without bringing attention to ourselves.

"We worked out this system. One whistle, they've spotted the snake, but he's not on our scent yet. Two whistles, the snake's on our scent. That's when I take out the snake charmer. Three whistles, I've hypnotized the beast. It's a system that has saved our lives for sure."

Horatio recalled Whimser telling him the snails "have helped us in our travels more than we can say." Now Horatio understood why.

"You should have sheen the look in that shnake'sh eyesh when he heard the mushic," said Mish, "His eyesh glazed over and hish tongue shtuck out on one shide like he wash shick. He jusht hung there in midair shwaying back and forth."

"How big a snake was it?" Horatio asked.

"About ash long ash ten of the Emblem staffsh put together," said Mish. "Poishonous too. Not the kind of shnake you'd want to get bit by."

Horatio chuckled nervously.

"I think we've gone far enough for today. We should camp here for tonight," said Whisklet. "It's going to get dark soon. We'll want to hike through Glob Swamp when it's daylight."

They dug a burrow and built a fire with twigs they found nearby. Whisklet took out the biscuits their mother had given them. There were ten biscuits altogether. "We'll each get one for tonight," said Whisklet, pointing to Whimser and Horatio. "Mish and Mosh you can share one. We'll save the rest."

"Why do *we* have to share?" asked Mish.

"Because you're smaller. And you don't need to eat so much."

"Who shaysh?"

"I do," said Whisklet, which silenced them.

The three small mammals bit into their biscuits. With the first taste, their eyes closed and a feeling of satisfaction came over them. "My, these are good," said Horatio.

"Nothing like these biscuits in all the land," said Whimser. They savored each bite.

Mish and Mosh eyed each other from across their biscuit. "Ready, set, go!" shouted Mish. Before Mosh could take even his third bite, Mish had gobbled up the whole biscuit. Mish gave a loud burp. Mosh glared at him.

Mosh slowly, glumly glided his way over to Horatio. "You didn't get much did you?" Horatio asked. Mosh shook his head. Horatio broke off some of his biscuit and gave it to him.

"Thanksh," Mosh whispered to him. "Shorry about eating your food the other day."

"Don't worry about it," Horatio whispered back.

They amused themselves in the early evening hours listening to Whimser's music, while Whisklet took out the rope and showed Horatio how to tie knots.

"You're a fast learner," Whisklet told him.

Sitting around the fire, as nighttime set in, Horatio asked a question that had been on his mind. "How will we cross the river to get to Francis Hopper?"

"We'll build a raft," said Whisklet.

"What's a raft?"

"A raft's a little boat made of sticks we tie together. It floats on the water. And we sit on top of it. But we can only use it after we get past the waterfall. The current is too fast upriver where we are. After the waterfall the current is calmer."

"Have you ever built a raft before?"

"Sure, we have. We've even used it to cross the river. Never took it downriver to the sea. But it's the fastest way to travel."

"The thing is," said Horatio, "I don't know how to swim."

"Then we'll have to make sure you don't fall off."

Chapter 8

Leala the Archer

Far away from the traveling companions, in a clearing in the forest near the sea, a father and a daughter hedgehog practiced for the Tournament of Archers.

"Bull's-eye!" shouted Leala's father, Wal. "That's 19 bull's-eyes out of 20 shots. Well done!"

"And I only missed the one because my nose twitched," said Leala.

"If you shoot like that during the tournament, you'll have a real chance of winning. Most archers wouldn't hit even ten in a row, never mind 19 out of 20."

"Except for Tran," said Leala.

"True, he's going to be the toughest competition you'll face this year. But even he would be hard-pressed to hit 19 out of 20. You've had a good practice. Really

good. Let's head on back."

This was Leala's final practice before she headed off for the tournament the next morning. She would be representing her village at the tournament, as she had won the Hedgehog Archery Championship earlier in the year. As they strolled back to the burrow, they could hear in the distance the ocean's waves against the shore. "I can't wait for the tournament. It's going to be a blast."

Her father laughed. "I remember when I went to the

tournament. That *was* a blast." Wal had been a champion archer in his day, but he rarely picked up a bow and arrow now.

A hawk's loud "SKEEEYAK" echoed through the forest. Wal and Leala shuddered. They picked up their pace. The edginess in the air brought their conversation to a halt.

"Dad?" Leala asked, breaking the silence.

"Yes?"

"Why don't we teach every hedgehog how to shoot a bow and arrow so they can protect themselves against hawks?"

Her father sighed. "Only a few hedgehogs can shoot a bow and arrow. You might think it's easy, but it's not. It's easy for you because you have a gift. And there are far more hawks than there are hedgehogs who are archers. Even those that can use a bow and arrow—like you and me—may not be able to hit a fast-moving hawk."

"I bet I could hit one," Leala boasted.

Wal stopped and stood in front of her. "Now listen to me. Listen carefully." He put his paws on her shoulders. "I don't want you to even try. Do you understand?"

"Uh-huh" said Leala, her face staring at the ground.

"Archery is a sport, a game. But shooting at a hawk is *not* a game. It's not about being brave or being a heroine. It's not about being a good enough shot. It's about being smart—smart enough to stay alive. Do you understand me?"

"Yes."

"I don't want you to make jokes like that again."

"All right, I *understand*." Her father tilted his face, his eyebrows raised. He still had not removed his paws from her shoulders. "I *do*, Dad. I understand. I do."

"All right, then." He finally smiled at her. "Just focus on the tournament," he laughed. "That's enough for you to think about."

When they got back to their burrow and crawled in, they could smell the wonderful aroma of blackberry cobbler. Leala's mother had prepared a special supper for them. She had invited two close friends of the family to join them for dinner. They were so close Leala called them uncle and aunt.

Uncle Finneus was a stocky hedgehog who managed the village's library of books, including their collection of rare books and antiquities. Like Leala's father, Uncle Finneus was a former champion archer himself. He was one of the few hedgehogs who had explored lands outside their village. Every once in a while he would bring back an ancient or unusual item for their collection.

Aunt Quillity was the matron of the village. Her eyesight was poor, and her paws weren't nearly as nimble as they were when she was younger. But she could still knit and embroider better than anyone. The clothing, blankets, and other objects she crafted were known to last for years without a thread or stitch needing to be redone.

"How was practice?" Leala's mother asked, as they sat around the table.

"Excellent, 19 out of 20 bull's-eyes," said Leala.

"I think you're ready. I really do," her mother told her.

"I do too," her father added.

"I won the Tournament of Archers by hitting seven bull's-eyes in a row," said Uncle Finneus. "It's amazing how much better kids are today. I can't imagine hitting 19 out of 20."

After supper, Uncle Finneus and Aunt Quillity took out a package. Leala's face lit up. She hadn't been expecting anything. "It's a going away present," said Aunt Quillity. "We thought you could use it."

She unwrapped the package to find a beautifully hand-sewn quiver for her arrows, made in purple cloth with the words "Leala the Archer" in gold curved letters across it.

"Thank you," Leala said. She reached down and gave Aunt Quillity a hug. A quiver of this quality would have honored any archer. "This will go with me wherever I go."

"We are so proud of you," Aunt Quillity told her.

Chapter 9

Globdum

As the sun rose the next morning, blurry in the mist, the traveling companions headed south, hiking in the direction of Glob Swamp. Mish rode atop Whimser's knapsack, but for the first time, Mosh rode atop Horatio's. Horatio was surprised and touched. It was a small thing—having this little snail pal sitting there—but it made Horatio feel like he was now really part of the gang.

"You know," Mosh said to Horatio, "there'sh an 'o' in both of our namesh."

"So there is," Horatio said. "I hadn't thought of that."

After about an hour's walk they could feel the ground underneath them becoming soggier. Now and then the "plop" of an acorn or twig falling from a tree onto the swampy ground accompanied the sounds of their feet squishing the damp earth. Cyprus trees began to appear, with their long pointy roots popping out of the soil.

"We need to keep a look out for any type of mud," said Whisklet.

The trees became so dense that the forest darkened, and it became hard for them to see the ground beneath them. They had hoped the daylight would help them spot any mud puddles—or quicksand disguised as mud puddles.

All of a sudden, Whisklet halted. "That's a small mud puddle right there," he pointed in front of them. "Mish, Mosh, is it just a puddle, or is it quicksand?"

The snails looked at the puddle carefully from atop the knapsacks. "It's jusht a mud puddle," Mish assured him.

"Absholutely, no queshtion about it," said Mosh.

Whimser took a small rock and tossed it into the puddle. It lay on the surface of the puddle for a second, and then sunk right through as it if were being sucked down. The quicksand seemed to make a gulping sound as the rock vanished.

"That's no mud puddle," said Whimser.

"It'sh not?" Mish and Mosh asked in unison.

"You said you were experts!" Whisklet threw up his arms.

"I guessh maybe we're jusht expertsh on mud, not quickshand," said Mosh.

An eerie dread crept into each of them. They had been counting on Mish and Mosh to help them navigate their way through this terrain.

They kept far away from the small spot of quicksand and stayed on the driest part of the swampy ground they could find. As they trudged on, a whole swath of land to their left grew muddier. Then a whole swath of land to their right became muddy as well. They followed their only remaining route, a narrow strip of dry land, until the trunk of a tall tree blocked their path.

"I didn't realize it was going to be this muddy," said Whimser.

They crawled around the tree's trunk to find a vast area of muddy ground stretched out ahead of them. The only dry area of land lay behind them, the narrow strip they had just traveled on. "We'll have to turn around," said Whisklet.

As they started to turn back, to their shock, the route of dry land—their escape route—had become muddy. Whether it was really mud or quicksand they couldn't tell. The muddy ground seemed to be spreading closer to them, moving fast. Then suddenly it formed into a large ball of mud and began thundering toward them. The boulder of mud picked up speed. The only place for them to go was up, to a high branch well off the ground. The huge ball of mud rolled straight into the tree. The tree shook hard, but the three small mammals and two snails held on.

"Ouch," it said. Then out of this formless ball of mud, a round faceless head appeared, and a solitary arm and hand stretched out from its side. The index finger of the hand extended outward, and rubbed the top of its head. "I think I hit my head," it said, although it had no mouth to utter the words.

"What in the world is that?" whispered Whisklet to the others.

Just as quickly, the head disappeared back into the mass of a ball, and two thin legs emerged. The now headless creature reached down with its arm and rubbed its right knee. "Or maybe I bumped my knee," it said. Then a head appeared again and the form of a mouth became visible for the first time, and it gave a loud bellow.

"What creatures are you up there?" It extended its long arm of mud, which seemed to grow effortlessly up the tree. Its index finger came right at them. "What do you feel like?" The small mammals could find nowhere to hide, as the index finger extended straight to Whisklet and touched him. "Oooh, furry," the creature said. It then reached up to touch Whimser. "Oooh, furry." Finally, it reached out to touch Horatio. Its index finger went straight through one of Horatio's spikes. "Oooh, pokey."

"Look!" whispered Whimser. "It's got eyes now." Another arm extended out of its torso ball. Its two hands seemed to grab both of its eyes and pull them straight out of their sockets.

The three small mammals turned their heads in disgust.

"Slimeeeey," said the creature. It put the eyes back on its head, one in the middle of what would have been its forehead, the other slightly to the right of where a nose normally would reside. It kept taking the eyes out of its head to rearrange them.

"That's the grossest thing I've ever seen," whispered Whisklet.

"Wait, those aren't real eyes!" exclaimed Whimser. "Those are Mish and Mosh!" He shouted at them, "Get back up here!"

The creature set on the tree what they had thought had been its eyes. "I want the pokey one," it said. It extended its arm upward again, its hand outstretched. Whimser and Whisklet readied themselves with their staffs to defend Horatio, although they had no idea what their staffs could do against this creature. They doubted it would have any understanding of the Emblems of Graysent.

Suddenly, they heard a voice, "Yo, cowboys, git 'n 'ere." They looked up and saw a small hole a few feet above them they hadn't noticed before. They scampered to the hole, and dived in right before the creature's hand closed around Horatio.

"Where'd you go?" they heard the creature call out.

"My squirrelly-whirl," exclaimed the squirrel inside the hole. "What are nice cowfolk like ya doin' 'round these parts? Follow me." The squirrel led them down the hollow of the tree until they came to another opening that led to a long tunnel inside a branch. "We'll take that," said the squirrel. "It'll lead us outta 'ere."The three small mammals remained fixed, still stunned. "Yo, cowpokes, let's move it!" the squirrel commanded.

They could see the creature's fingers poking into the hole, and one of the fingers seemed to grow longer and longer as it reached down toward them.

"Fast!" said the squirrel. The mammals fled through the tunnel inside the branch.

"We're traveling with some snails," said Whimser.

"Ain't no time to wait."

"We won't need to," said Whimser. Sure enough, Mish and Mosh had caught up with them inside the branch. "*There* you are."

They reached the opening at the end of the branch, and were now only a short jump away from a nearby tree. Mish snuck inside Whimser's knapsack and Mosh snuck inside Horatio's. All the mammals made the leap and landed safely on the other tree. "It'll take him a while to figure out where we went. You off to a rodeo?" the squirrel asked.

"No, why?" asked Whimser.

"What's with the hats?"

Whimser had wondered why the squirrel had kept calling them cowboys and cowpoke. "We wear these when we go hiking or camping."

Whimser's answer seemed to make as much sense to the squirrel, as if Whimser had told him they put on beards when they go camping.

"What kind of creature is that?" asked Whisklet.

"That's Globdum. He's made 'tirely outta mud. Can change into 'most any shape 'n size. He can git tall as a tree or wide as a swamp. He ain't all mean. He jus ain't fig'rd out mos folk can't breathe if they git swallowed up by mud."

Down below them, the ground was muddy for as far as they could see. "What are we going to do? We can't get across this land when it's covered with mud and quicksand," said Whisklet.

"We fly," said the squirrel.

"If we had wings."

"We do." The squirrel extended his paws to show the webbing in his fur. "I'm a flyin' squirrel. Latch is the name. Git on 'n 'old tight."

Whisklet and Whimser put the Emblems under the top flaps of their knapsacks, and tied the flaps down tight. Horatio climbed onto the middle of Latch's back with Whimser on his left and Whisklet on his right. They both kept one paw on Horatio's knapsack to make sure he didn't fall off. Mish and Mosh slimed back into the knapsacks. They didn't want to see what was about to happen.

"No eating our food," Whimser warned them. But this was one of those rare moments when neither Mish nor Mosh cared about food.

Horatio dug his paws into Latch's fur as hard as he could.

"Y'all ready?" Latch asked.

Whisklet and Whimser looked at each other and at Horatio. They all nodded. "Ready," said Whisklet.

With one big leap, Latch sailed through the air, taking

on speed through the trees. The wind rushed by them, making their hats flap. The small mammals could do nothing else but hold on, and hope for a soft landing—that's not what they got. Latch hit the tree hard, and held on fast, but the sudden stop jerked Horatio right off. Whisklet and Whimser, whose paws were holding tightly to his knapsack, held him aloft. Horatio's hat flew off his head and floated topsy-turvily to the ground. Horatio scrambled back on board Latch's back. They all watched the hat hit the ground and disappear in an instant, followed by a loud gulp.

"That was quicksand," said Whisklet.

Horatio was crestfallen. "I'm so sorry about your hat."

"Don't worry. Better to lose your hat than your life. But that's another reason to hold on," said Whimser. "If the fall doesn't kill you, the quicksand will."

"I'll go for a softa landin' next time 'round," said Latch. "I ain't used to critters on my back."

Latch didn't really fly; he glided. He had landed on the tree much lower to the ground than where they had started—so low that they thought Globdum might grab them up. They all had to scamper up the tree to give Latch enough height to take another leap.

"OK, 'old on, 'ere we go," Latch called out. He took off with a leap—again the mammals soared through the air, the wind in their faces. And when Latch landed this time, none of them were jarred loose.

Three more leaps—three more times scampering up

the trees after they landed—and though each leap caused a small gallop in the pit of the riders' stomachs, every leap ended in a solid, safe landing.

On the sixth leap, Latch overshot the tree, and grabbed hold of a branch instead. Had Latch been flying solo this would not have mattered. But with the added weight, the branch sent them careening straight toward the ground—all of them sure they were hurling right into quicksand. But the branch stopped just short and sprang back up like a bungee cord. It bounced up and down several terrifying times before coming to a halt.

"I guess I can't land on branches neither," said Latch.

Whisklet asked, "Have you ever missed a tree or branch and ended up falling to the ground?"

"Never," said Latch. Whisklet breathed a sigh of relief.

"Have you ever carried three riders on your back before?" Whisklet asked.

"Never," said Latch, and Whisklet's sense of relief dissolved away.

Soon, though, all of the animals had become expert at flying through the air. Latch now always stuck the landing solidly on the trunk of a tree, never needing to reach for a branch, never setting down too hard, and never jerking any of his riders loose. They finally reached the edge of Glob Swamp, looked down, and could see dry ground beneath them.

"We did it!" Whimser exclaimed. Mish and Mosh climbed out of the knapsacks to take a look. "We made it."

"Now what y'all doing in these parts?"

"We're going to one of the swimming holes beyond the waterfall."

"I never go that far. I'm just a simple swamp squirrel. I can take ya as far as the waterfall, but ya won't get there today."

"That's all right," said Whisklet. "Now that we're out of Glob Swamp, we'll probably camp somewhere here."

"I wouldn't camp no where near here on the ground. If ya want, ya can stay at my place, I got a pad high up in a tree. But if ya wanna get there 'fore dark, we got to fly some more."

"Everyone okay to keep flying?" asked Whisklet.

"Call me a flying hamster!" exclaimed Whimser.

"Let's fly!" said Horatio.

They all grabbed hold of Latch. Mish and Mosh groaned and slimed their way back into the knapsacks again. "I threw up five times already," said Mish.

Whimser's eyes grew wide. "In my *knapsaaack*!" his yell echoed through the air as Latch leapt to the next tree.

Chapter 10

Horatio's Gift

Twenty-two leaps later, Latch stopped. "Y'all can git off now. This is the tree where I live."

High up on the tree, hidden in the foliage, was a deep hole. "Welcome to my home. This hole's been in my family since my great-grandpaw was a boy. My paw, grandpaw, and great-grandpaw all lived here. And now me."

Inside the hole, a huge cavernous space spread out before them, the flooring full of soft feathers and pine needles.

"There's plenty o' room. Make yourselves comf'table." Latch then noticed the Emblems. "What are those?"

"They're the Emblems of Graysent," Whimser told him.

"You're from the Forest of Epoh?"

"That's right."

"And are friends of Graysent the Owl?"

Whisklet and Whimser nodded.

"I'll be. I never 'spected friends of Graysent would be coming my way."

"Well, we're much obliged to you for your help," said Whisklet.

"To tell ya the truth, I didn't notice the Emblems at first. I couldn't git over your hats." Whimser honked. Latch took a step back. "With a laugh like that ya could be a gander." Whimser honked again. "One proud gander," Latch kept at him.

Whimser was now honking so loudly they all burst out laughing. Except for Horatio, who was staring at an object hanging on the far wall of Latch's home—it was a bow.

"Looks like our little hedgehog has found somethin'," said Latch. "Ya an archer?"

"No," Horatio blushed. "Just curious. It brings back a memory, a faraway memory. I can't really recall it."

"Have ya ever shot one?"

"No, not that I remember."

"Not that ya can remember? What do ya mean?"

Horatio stumbled on the words.

"He's a Solety," said Whimser softly.

Horatio's ears turned red again.

"Well, the bow on the wall is one I use. It's too big for ya. But I've another I used when I was littler. I'll git it."

Latch opened up a large chest with an ornate golden latch. "My paw made this chest for me right before I'as born. Put this golden latch on it. Then they gave me the name Latch. Everythin' from my youngun days, I keep in 'ere."

He took out a bow and a quiver of arrows and handed the bow to Horatio. Horatio pulled the string taut and held it up in one fluid motion, as if he had been shooting arrows every day of his life.

"Something tells me it's not the first time ya held a bow."

"It seems to come naturally."

"Heck, maybe ya got some archery in ya blood," said Latch. "Morrow mornin', we'll see if ya can shoot it."

"Where?" Horatio looked around the cavernous home.

"Outside," Latch laughed. "This place ain't that big." Whimser honked again. "Don't git started on me," he chuckled at Whimser.

Before they went to bed, Whisklet took out some of the pecan tart their mother had given them and shared it with Latch. "Mighty fine," said Latch, after eating his piece. "Now I think we need some shut-eye."

They settled down for the night. Horatio dreamed of arrows flying into stars.

The next morning, they all climbed out of the hole and down the tree to the ground. Horatio slung the bow around his shoulder, while Latch held on to the arrows.

"Let's find ya a good target," Latch said, looking around. "There! Ya see that knot in the tree o'er there. It's not too far a shot, but a small target. See how close ya can git to it. I'll show ya how to set the arrow."

"I think I know how to set the arrow."

Latch handed him an arrow, and they all stood behind Horatio. In one swift motion, Horatio set the arrow, pulled back the bow, and fired. The arrow hit the knot dead center.

"Holy cow!" said Whimser.

They all stared at Horatio, stunned. Whisklet and Whimser had the same dumbfounded expression they had when they first saw Horatio.

"That some kinda magic trick?" asked Latch.

"I don't know magic," said Horatio.

"Where did you learn how to shoot like that?" asked Whisklet.

"I don't know," Horatio shrugged. "I just can."

Latch's expression changed. "Well, I said ya might got some archery blood in ya. But strip the fur off my tail! I ain't never seen that. Try it again."

Horatio took another arrow, set it, pulled back and fired. It brushed the first arrow and hit the knot dead center again.

No one spoke. No one even uttered a sound.

Finally, Latch got some words out. "That's jus spooky. Y'all tryin' to pull a fast one on me?"

"What makes you say that?" asked Whisklet.

"Well, I know friends of Graysent ain't travelin' in these parts to visit a swimmin' hole. I may be simple, but I know which way to fly. And your hedgehog friend 'ere says he's never shot in his life and then shoots like a sharpshooter. What's goin' on?"

"I honestly don't know how I did it. I must have been taught but can't remember."

Latch grunted as if to say he believed Horatio. He turned to Whisklet. "So, start talkin'. What kinda trip ya really on?"

The three small mammals looked from one to another, not sure how much they should say. "Tell him," Whisklet whispered to Horatio. "The whole story."

Horatio started from the beginning. He told Latch about Rollic, the sound of the river inside him, and about Scarretchen.

A long time passed before Latch spoke. "If I didn't know better, I'd say ya tell a good tale. But I know somethin' about the sound ya hear. A couple years 'go a good friend o' mine, a flyin' squirrel like me, but olda, had a small boy disappear. Next day he heard a sound like ya do. Not the sound o' the river, but o' the wind rushin' by him—the sound ya heard when we flew through the trees. He knew for sure it was his boy callin' to him too. He set off to find him. Never came back. This ol' swamp ain't been the same without 'em."

"I'm sorry to hear that," said Whisklet.

"Maybe what happened to your otter friend, happened to my friend and his boy. If ya really set on findin' ya friend, y'all need all the help ya can git."

"You could come with us."

"No, as I said, I'm a simple swamp squirrel. Never been 'way from my hole for long. Wouldn't want some other critter movin' in. To tell ya the truth, I don't think I'd the courage to take on a creature like Scarretchen."

"I don't know if I have the courage either," said Horatio. "I just need to save my friend."

Latch smiled. He handed Horatio the quiver of arrows. "Take the bow and arrows with ya. They might help. And if ya do find out anythin' 'bout my friend, come back and tell me."

"I will," said Horatio.

"Well, I said I'd take ya as far as the waterfall. It ain't far from here. Let's git movin'." He walked over to the knot in the tree and pulled out the arrows. Then he stuck them back in Horatio's quiver. "We still ain't figured out how ya learned to shoot like that."

Horatio's face beamed. He couldn't help it. He shrugged. "I don't have a clue," he said with a grin that wouldn't leave his face. He couldn't wait to try it again.

Chapter 11

The Painted Turtles

The three small mammals followed Latch through the woods into a clearing on a high cliff. "There it is," said Latch, pointing below them to a massive waterfall. "It's a steep climb down to the river. So go slow. From there it's a short hike to the swimmin' hole ya lookin' for."

"We've been to the swimming hole before," said Whisklet. "We'll be able to find it."

"I'll leave ya here, then."

"Thanks again," said Horatio, "for saving our lives—and for the bow and arrows."

"Make good use of 'em."

Whisklet and Whimser shook his paw. "Thank you. If you ever do set your mind on traveling, come to the Forest of Epoh. You'll always be welcome," Whisklet told him.

As they worked their way down the cliff to the river, the spray from the waterfall reached them. "This must be the waterfall Rollic fell over," thought Horatio. He couldn't believe he was seeing it with his own eyes. In his home by the riverbank, he never imagined traveling this far.

When they reached the bank of the river, they could see the river had formed a gentle pool of water just beyond the waterfall. Logs that had been carried downriver, over the waterfall, collided and intertwined with one another, and came to a halt in the pool. Painted turtles sunbathed on the logs.

"If anyone might have spotted Rollic, it would have been one of the turtles," said Whisklet. "If they saw him here, then we know he wouldn't have met up with Scarretchen until later."

"Excuse me, could you help us?" Whisklet called out to the relaxing turtles, who gave no reply.

Whimser tried again, "Excuse me, we're in need of assistance."

Now Horatio tried, "I'm looking for my friend, who's missing."

They still didn't answer.

"Do they talk a different language?" asked Horatio.

"No," said Whisklet. "Turtles understand our language. They are one of the few reptiles that do."

Mish tried his high-pitched whistle. Horatio had

to cover his ears. But the turtles seemed completely undisturbed. "I don't think turtles can hear your whistle," said Whimser.

Whisklet set down his hat, "Maybe I'll just have to swim out there. The current seems calm enough here." He jumped in. They could tell he was not a natural swimmer, but he made dogged progress out to the closest log floating in the pool.

"Excuse me," he said to one of the turtles. Treading water wasn't easy. His head sank below the surface for a brief second, and he came back up sputtering, "Ooze ee."

The turtles began to notice now. "Who's the oddball?" one turtle said to his neighbor on the log.

"It looks like a mouse in the water is trying to say something," said the other.

Whisklet, encouraged that he had their attention, held himself up in the water as fully as he could, "I'm a hamster," and his head went below the surface a second time before coming back up.

"He says he's a hamster."

"What would a hamster be doing in the middle of the river? They don't swim."

"'Cusee," Whimser managed to utter before going under again.

"Well, why would a mouse swim out here and say he's a hamster?"

"Blee, blee," Whisklet blubbered as he came back up only to go back under.

"Well, at least a mouse can swim. A hamster can't. So between the two, the odds are better it's a mouse."

"Me!" Whisklet tried one more time.

"They're ignoring him!" said Whimser frantically. He jumped in, hat and all, to go after him. But he started flailing away once he realized the water was over his head. Horatio hurriedly tried to get the rope out of his knapsack to rescue Whimser, but it was hopelessly tangled up.

"But he doesn't look like much of a swimmer, so he could be a hamster," the turtle continued the debate. Then, for the first time, the turtle noticed Whisklet couldn't keep his head from dropping below the surface. "Oh, bother. Why is it turtles always have to rescue animals who can't swim?" The turtle plopped off the log and swam over to Whisklet, so he could rest on his back.

"Thank you, so much," he said, gasping for breath. "I'm hoping," he gasped. "You can," he gasped again. "Help me."

"He looks like a hamster," said the turtle calling to his friend, who remained fixed to the log.

"He looks like just another waterlogged fur ball, if you ask me. What was he doing in the river in the first place?"

Whisklet ignored the snide remark and tried again, "I'm hoping you can help me."

"I can rescue your friend," the turtle beneath him replied.

Whisklet only then realized Whimser had jumped in after him. "Yes! Hurry!"

The turtle picked up the flailing Whimser on his way back.

"My hat," Whimser wheezed, as he reached down from atop the turtle to pluck it out of the water.

Horatio was still trying to get the rope untangled.

"We're looking for a missing otter, and were wondering if he came this way," Whisklet asked.

"I've not seen an otter for days," the turtle said. He dropped Whisklet and Whimser off, and turned around.

"Wait!" cried Whisklet, but the turtle ignored him. "Well, I never ...," Whisklet huffed, as the turtle swam back to the log to sunbathe again. Whisklet and Whimser were dripping wet and had nothing to show for it. Horatio remained the only dry one, and felt somewhat guilty about the whole episode.

"We need a way to get their attention," said Whimser.

"I know!" shouted Horatio. He took out one of the biscuits from Whisklet's knapsack. "Why don't we throw biscuit crumbs on the water? That should get their attention."

"Brilliant!" exclaimed Whisklet.

"Would anyone like some biscuit?" Horatio shouted out. The dropping biscuit bits piqued the turtles' curiosity. First a lone turtle, then a second, then a third approached the shore where the bits of biscuit were landing.

"This is delicious," one turtle said. Soon, almost all of

the turtles had lumbered off their logs, and were scrapping around, trying to snag a piece. They were so focused on getting the biscuit crumbs that Horatio couldn't get them to listen. He stopped throwing anything more. At that moment, thirty pairs of turtle eyes stared back at him.

"There's more here, but I need to talk to you first,' Horatio explained. "My friend has been missing for a few days. He's a young otter, all brown, with two white front paws. His name is Rollic."

"I know the otter with white paws," called out one turtle.

"You do? When did you see him last?" Horatio asked.

"A few days ago. He was swimming by here. Downriver. But I don't know where he was going."

"Did anyone see him swimming back?"

The turtles all shook their heads.

"How about tossing some more of that biscuit you're holding into the water."

Horatio broke the remaining biscuit into small pieces. The turtles' heads bobbed up and down. "Can anyone tell me anything more about the otter?" Horatio asked. The turtles now shook their heads. With that Horatio threw the rest of the biscuit bits into the river. The turtles scrapped and fought for any crumb they could get.

"We still don't know how Rollic might have gotten captured," Whisklet said to the group, "but we know it would have happened after he passed by here. Maybe at the swimming hole. Scarretchen might have turned himself into some type of animal who visits swimming holes, so no one would recognize him. Maybe even another otter. Let's be careful who we talk to and what we say when we get there. Scarretchen might have come back for another victim."

Horatio put the rope he had now untangled neatly into his knapsack. Whisklet and Whimser wrung the water out of their shirts. Whimser squeezed the water out of his hat too.

They hiked along the river past a long stretch of cattails, a route Whisklet and Whimser had traveled before, toward the swimming hole. The sun started to get warm, and the hamsters felt themselves begin to dry off.

"Whimser?" Another question kept troubling Horatio.

"Yeah?"

"If my parents were pioneers, like you said, and had left the village to start a new life, do you think they would have left with a group or gone on their own?"

"Probably in a group. I don't think they would have set off on their own."

"But if they left with a group, how did I get separated from the whole group? Even if something did happen to my parents?"

"Hmm, maybe they left on their own, then," Whimser said. He had to admit Horatio had a good point. He couldn't see how Horatio would have ended up by himself, separated from a whole group.

"But then why did they leave on their own? Just the

two of them. Do you think they were kicked out? Did my father commit a crime or something and they were forced to leave?"

"I doubt they were kicked out," said Whimser. "Two criminal hedgehogs—a mom, and a dad, and their little kid—on the run," he joked. But he could see Horatio didn't find it humorous.

"But if my father did get kicked out for some reason, would my village take me, his son, back, if I wanted to return?"

"What makes you think that?" asked Whisklet. "What makes you think your father might have been kicked out of the village?"

"I don't know if that's what happened. But something must have happened."

"Would you want to visit your village and find out? After we rescue Rollic, I mean."

"Sure, if they'll have me."

Chapter 12

The Encounter

The afternoon turned out to be particularly hot, and the swimming hole was packed with animals: beavers, muskrats, otters, squirrels, chipmunks, raccoons, rabbits, and birds too numerous to count.

The sight of two hamsters carrying the Emblems of Graysent, and a hedgehog with a bow and quiver of arrows, caught everyone's attention. Whisklet realized if Scarretchen was somewhere in this throng of animals, he would certainly have noticed them.

Some came right up to Horatio and presumed he was in the Tournament of Archers. "Good luck to you tomorrow," a chipmunk said.

"I'm not in the tournament," Horatio explained. "When is it?"

"Tomorrow morning."

"We made it just in time," said Whisklet.

On the far side a stream fed into the swimming hole, creating a fast waterfall slide. Several young otters took turns going down it. "Let's see if they know anything," Whisklet said.

"What happens if one of them is Scarretchen in disguise?" asked Whimser. "How do we know if it's a real otter?"

"We'll watch them go down the slide first," said Whisklet. "Scarretchen doesn't seem like the kind of fellow who'd be here to have fun. Whichever otter seems to be having the most fun, we'll take that otter aside and talk to him."

One young otter screamed with glee as he came down the slide and made a huge splash. As he was shaking himself off, Whisklet nodded to Whimser. Whimser whispered to the otter, "We have a question for you."

"For me?" the young otter was surprised that visitors carrying the Emblems of Graysent would want to talk to him.

"Yeah, come here for a second."

The otter bounded over. "What's up?"

"Do you know an otter with front white

paws? Have you seen him before?"

"No."

"Okay, go on then."

The young otter sprinted off to get back in line for the waterfall. An athletic otter the color of bark went down the slide twirling over and over as he slid down. "Only a real otter would twirl like that," said Horatio. "Rollic used to do that in the river."

"Hey,"Whisklet called to the otter. "Got a question for you."

"Sure," he said as he sauntered over to them. "What did you think of my slide?" he asked. "Four complete twirls before I hit the water."

"Do you know an otter with front white paws?"

"Sure, he was here a few days ago. I come here just about every day."

Their eyes grew wide. "Do you know where he went?"

"Well, it was getting dark and we needed to leave. He was still here when we left."

"He's not supposed to come home after dark," said Horatio. "What was he doing the last time you saw him?"

"We were almost into the woods, and I turned and saw him talking to a beaver in the distance. A really big beaver."

"Is that beaver here now? Could you point him out for us?"

"Don't know for sure." He looked all around the swimming hole. "That might be him," he said pointing to the other side of the swimming hole. There on the grass a sizable beaver lay on his back, gnawing at a piece of wood. "He sometimes goes down the slide too."

"Thanks," they told the otter.

They made their way around the swimming hole. "What if the beaver is Scarretchen?" Whimser asked, stopping in his tracks. "What if he turns us into something?"

"He won't try anything like that out in the open, with all these other animals around," said Whisklet. "Let's just play it cool. Walk up to him real slow. Take it easy."

They came up to the beaver so quietly that the beaver didn't even notice them standing next to him. "We'd like a word with you," said Whisklet, lowering his voice.

The beaver lifted his head, and squinted into the sun. He couldn't quite make out who was speaking to him. He placed a paw over his eyes and saw the Emblems clearly now. The beaver jumped up quickly. He towered over the smaller mammals but still seemed very nervous.

"Certainly," he said. "How can I help you?"

"Did you have a conversation with an otter with white front paws a few days ago?"

"An otter?"

"It was early in the evening, near the waterfall slide."

"Yes, yes," the beaver replied, "I do recall a conversation with an otter with white paws. Some young otters had left for the day, and I decided to take a turn down the slide. This otter—the one with the white paws—was telling me what a fun day he had."

"Did he tell you anything else?"

"He mentioned his friend Horatio. He said his friend Horatio would have loved it here, but he lives far up north and he's just a small hedgehog, so it would be too far for him to travel." At that moment the beaver noticed the name on Horatio's knapsack. "Is that you?" he asked Horatio.

"Yes," Horatio told him.

"You don't say," the beaver became more animated. "I remember the conversation because I told him I didn't think any hedgehogs lived upriver from here. I actually thought he might be making it up."

"Where did the otter go after you spoke with him?"

"I'm not sure. I had walked to the top of the slide. A couple of other animals were ahead of me. I noticed a muskrat had come up to the otter. I could hear their conversation clearly. I remember the muskrat saying, 'You're a friend of Horatio? I think I know your friend Horatio's father.'"

"My father!" Horatio exclaimed.

"And then the otter said, 'I didn't know he had a father.'"

"And the muskrat said, 'Yes, his father borrowed one of my wishing stones. They grant any wish you want." Then the otter said kind of jokingly, 'Well, I wish I could get back home before dark.' That's all I heard of their conversation. I went down the slide, and when I got out of the water, I saw the muskrat and otter walking together into the woods toward the river."

"Do you see that same muskrat here today?"

"I can't tell. He was just your ordinary muskrat. Nothing special."

"Thanks. This has been helpful."

The three small mammals huddled together. "Scarretchen knew my father?" Horatio whispered. He still couldn't believe it. "That must have been Scarretchen disguised as the muskrat."

"Do you trust this beaver?" asked Whisklet.

"He seemed convincing to me," said Whimser.

"Maybe Rollic went with the muskrat to make a wish," said Horatio. "To get home before dark." He shook his head at the thought.

"And maybe Scarretchen chose Rollic to get to you," said Whisklet.

"What do you mean?"

"Maybe your father didn't borrow one of his wishing stones. He took one. Maybe he fled the village because Scarretchen was after him."

Horatio nodded. It all made sense to him. "And Scarretchen is having Rollic call to me. To get me to come. He wants to capture me to get back at my father."

They stayed huddled together without another word. It now dawned on them. Scarretchen hadn't captured Rollic for the fun of it, as a game. Scarretchen was after revenge. Scarretchen was after Horatio.

Chapter 13

Building the Raft

"What do we do now?" asked Horatio.

"We build the raft," said Whisklet. "Fastest way to get down the river. We'll let it dry overnight and tomorrow morning while we go to the tournament. By the time the tournament is over, the raft should be ready to use."

"What do you mean dry it overnight?"

"We make it out of sticks from the forest and glue them together. The glue needs to dry before we set it in the water."

"Where do we get the glue?"

Whisklet smiled. "Another little trick we learned from Mish and Mosh."

"We ushe shlime," said Mish. "When we jusht ushe

shlime it makesh thingsh shlippery."

"But when we combine shlime and mud together," said Mosh, "it becomesh like glue when it driesh. Keepsh the shticksh tight together—watertight."

"We'll need about twelve sticks, all the same height," said Whisklet. "Each stick should be twice as tall as us. And each should be about the same width too—about half as wide as us. That should be wide enough for the three of us to float on, with room to spare."

They canvassed the woods searching for the sticks and twigs that matched Whisklet's dimensions. One by one they brought them down to the riverside. Then they took ivy they found in the woods and around the base of trees. They stripped the ivy of its leaves leaving just the sinewy vine. They tied the sticks together—under and over each one—with the strips of vine. Then Mish and Mosh slimed the raft up and down between the sticks, while the three mammals spread mud over the slime. As the mud and slime combined, they could feel it getting stickier.

A squirrel stopped by to watch them work. "What ya doing?"

"Building a raft."

"What ya going to do with it?"

"Take it downriver."

"How far?" he asked, stuffing an acorn in his mouth.

"All the way to the sea."

He gagged and bits of acorn spit out of his mouth, "All the way to the sea!"

When word got around, more animals stopped by to watch them work. None of them had seen small mammals assemble a raft before. And no one had ever heard of small mammals going downriver all the way to the sea.

Some of the painted turtles came out of the river to see what the crowd was gawking at. They weren't surprised to see the three small mammals at the center of it. "Got any more biscuits?" asked one turtle.

"We have some pecan tart," said Whisklet. He didn't want to give away any more biscuits. He was looking forward to saving the biscuits for later.

"That sounds good," said the turtle.

"If you help us out," said Whisklet.

"What do you need?"

"Watch our raft overnight. Make sure no one steals it."

"Not a problem."

When the final touches of slime and mud had been spread over the raft, and they made the last final tug to tighten the vines, they stood back to look at their workmanship.

"That's one strong raft," said Whisklet.

"Strongest one we've ever made," said Whimser.

"How many rafts have you made?" asked Horatio.

"Well, we've only made one other raft. But this one is stronger."

"It will take us downriver," assured Whisklet. "We just need to let it dry."

Each turtle crawled up onto the raft and took a corner.

"We'll sleep here tonight," a turtle told them. "Don't worry. It will be right here when you get back."

"Thanks," said Whisklet.

Horatio couldn't see how the turtles would defend the raft against a thief.

"All they need to do is sit there," said Whisklet. "A small mammal who wanted the raft would have to find a way to budge them off. And no small mammal is strong enough to do that. A larger mammal could, but a raft this size would be of no use to a large mammal."

"That's why turtles are great guards," said Whimser. "They don't even need to stay awake."

Chapter 14

The Tournament of Archers

Horatio rose bright and early the next morning in their burrow. He couldn't wait to get to the Tournament of Archers. Everyone else was still asleep. "Let's see what we have for breakfast," he said, making as much noise as he could. Mish and Mosh came at once. "Too bad you guys don't chew loudly," he told them. "That would wake them up."

"No, but we can do shomething elshe," Mosh said. He pushed his face into Horatio's fur, pulled it out, and gave one humongous sneeze, "HOOOF!"

Whisklet and Whimser jumped up with a start.

"Too much fur makesh my noshe tickle," he told Horatio.

"I didn't know snails could sneeze."

"Well, we're not your ushual shnailsh."

"Breakfast time!" Horatio called out to the sleepy hamsters. "We've got biscuits, hazelnuts, blueberries. What do you guys want?"

"Umm," said Whisklet yawning. "Some blueberries would be good this morning."

After breakfast they quickly checked on their raft—the turtles were still sleeping soundly on top of it—and then hurried off to the tournament grounds. They were met by scores and scores of mammals heading the same way.

"It's going to be packed," said Whimser.

"Good thing we didn't get here any later," said Horatio.

They picked up the pace, and found some seats on the grandstand four rows from the front. They lowered the Emblems so other animals could see behind them. To their right sat a marmot with a green felt hat. To their left sat a raccoon wearing a vest covered with pockets.

In front of them, eight targets stood in a row, far from the grandstand, in the open field of the tournament grounds. Behind a bright yellow line near the grandstand were eight stands to hold the archers' quivers and eight chairs.

A tall black curtain with an opening in the middle hung from a huge wooden frame. On either side of the opening, the curtain displayed a flaming arrow in orange embroidery. Horatio suspected the archers were waiting behind the curtain. The curtain stood near a long table with a red tablecloth. At the table sat six badgers. Two of the badgers were dressed to the hilt in top hats and formal suits. The remaining four badgers carried bows and arrows on their muscular shoulders and wore black jackets.

"Who are the badgers?" asked Horatio.

The marmot on Horatio's right explained, "The ones with the top hats are the announcer and the tournament judge. The ones with bows are the bodyguards for the archers. They pick up archers from their villages and escort them here. That way the archers stay safe from predators. Even for small mammals who are expert archers, it's dangerous to travel alone."

"Do the small mammals have to walk all the way here?"

"No, the badgers transport them here in one of the Grand Wagons. See that one at the far end of the grandstand?" Horatio noticed it now. It was ornately painted in orange and yellow spirals with two large wheels in the back and two long poles to pull it. "The badgers go from village to village and pick up the small mammals who are headed for the tournament. If a small mammal had to travel on foot the whole way, he'd be too worn out to compete."

"Is the hedgehog champion going to be here?"

"Oh, I'm sure he is. Hedgehogs compete in this tournament every year. And they often win."

Horatio scanned the rest of the animals in the grandstands. He could only see a few small mammals—there were no other hedgehogs. Horatio thought to himself, "I guess the only small mammals who come to the tournament must live nearby."

As the crowd settled down, one of the badgers with a top hat finally stood up. He spoke in a loud voice, "We welcome you to the 127th Annual Tournament of Archers." The audience cheered. "We have gathered here this year the finest assembly of archers we have seen in many years." The cheer turned into a roar. "And now I would like to introduce the archers themselves." The animals now stood up and roared again, before settling back down.

"Shooting in position 1, Meerstud the Mink." The mink ran through the opening in the black curtain, raised one paw as the crowd applauded, and bowed. He wore a white shirt with frills on the sleeves and sleek black pants.

"Shooting in position 2, Tran the Gray Squirrel. The crowd erupted in loud applause as Tran ran through the curtain.

"He must be good," whispered Horatio. Tran wore a pointed tan hat with a hawk's feather sticking out of it. His shirt sleeves and pants legs were frayed at the edges.

"He's a crowd favorite," the marmot whispered back. "Tran's been here before. If anyone can beat the hedgehog champion, Tran can."

The badger announced a marten, a weasel, and an ermine next. Then there seemed to be a bit longer pause before the announcer spoke again. The audience began to buzz with excitement.

"Shooting in position 6, Leala the Hedgehog." The crowd erupted with the loudest applause of the day. "She's

The 127th Tournament
of Archers

a girl!" exclaimed Horatio. "I didn't think of that." Leala strode through the curtain. She wore a matching purple cloak and pants with a gold stripe running down her pant legs. On her back she held the purple quiver with the words *Leala the Archer* in gold. Horatio could hardly believe his eyes. "She's beautiful," he said in a loud whisper, only to get shoved by Whisklet and Whimser from both sides.

"Is our little friend smitten?" kidded Whisklet.

Horatio blushed. "No, it's just I've never seen another hedgehog before."

"And never one so pretty."

"No," Horatio insisted, "I mean ...," but he was at a loss for words.

Finally, the announcer introduced the last two contestants, a grasshopper mouse and a ferret. All eight archers stood testing their bows or waving to the crowd.

The announcer continued: "We shall now explain the tournament rules. A round begins when at least one archer hits a bull's-eye. Any archers who have not hit a bull's-eye in that round have one more chance to do so. If they fail to do so, they are eliminated, and the next round begins. The rounds continue in this manner until only one archer remains. That archer is the Tournament of Archers *champion*." The audience cheered heavily at hearing the word *champion*. "We now begin round one. Archers—you may fire when ready."

In a split second, the archers raised their bows and fired. Horatio heard eight consecutive 'thunk, thunk, thunks.' Looking down the field he could see arrows in the bull's-eyes of all the targets but one.

Leala's shot was a perfect bull's-eye, as was every other archer except for the grasshopper mouse, who scolded himself. All the archers sat back down, setting their quivers on the stand next to them, leaving the grasshopper mouse the only contestant standing. That seemed to fluster the mouse even more. He had one more shot to hit a bull's-eye to stay in the tournament—he missed again. He walked off in a huff.

"Archers, please retrieve your arrows," said the announcer. When they had returned, "We now begin the second round."

Again Leala's second shot hit the bull's-eye. But this time two other contestants failed to do so, the marten and the ermine. On their second shots, the marten stayed in the tournament after hitting a bull's-eye, but the ermine missed badly and was out of the match.

"We begin the third round," said the announcer. Round after round, contestants fell out. Leala looked as calm as she had at the beginning—every shot a bull's-eye.

When they entered the twelfth round, there were only three contestants left: Leala, Tran, and Meerstud. Leala and Tran had never missed a bull's-eye. Meerstud had stayed in several times by hitting the bull's-eye on his second-chance shots. Tran winked at Leala. She did not look back.

"Archers, ready your bow. You may fire when ready."

Leala and Tran hit their bull's-eyes. But Meerstud missed. Then, on his second-chance shot, Meerstud missed again. "Ohhh," cried the crowd. Meerstud gave the crowd a deep bow and waved his paw elaborately as the audience applauded. That left just Leala and Tran for the championship.

Neither of them looked like they would ever miss. Leala had never competed against anyone as tough as Tran.

"With just two archers left in the competition, the championship rules now apply," said the announcer. "There are no second-chance shots in the championship rounds. In any round, if one archer shoots a bull's-eye, but the other archer does not, the archer who has shot the bull's-eye will be the champion. Archers, retrieve your arrows."

Leala and Tran walked side by side to the targets.

"You look really good," said Tran.

"Thanks. You're looking pretty good yourself."

"You're shooting pretty good too," he grinned. Leala shook her head. "So what's the highest number of bull's-eyes you've shot in a row?"

"At my last practice, I hit 19 out of 20. I only missed the one because my nose twitched."

"The last practice for me, I shot 25 in a row." They had reached the targets, and split up to retrieve their arrows. "I didn't make it 26," he called to her from his target, as he pulled out his arrow and looked at it admiringly. "Because I stopped after 25," he laughed.

When they returned to the yellow shooting line, they

both readied their bows. "Good luck," Tran said, as he turned to her and wiggled his nose.

Leala took a deep breath. "He's got a lot of confidence," she thought.

Eight rounds later, Leala and Tran had shot an amazing 20 straight bull's-eyes. The crowd knew they were witnessing a level of competition unseen in years. Tran no longer bothered to wink at Leala or even glance her way. The swagger had left him several rounds ago. Leala's calm and poise had vanished too. They both looked exhausted.

Finally, on the 21st round, Tran shot first and missed. The crowd gasped. Tran covered his face in his paws. He sat down dejectedly.

Leala needed to hit a bull's-eye to win. She simply needed to do what she had done in 20 straight rounds before. She pulled the bow back, took a deep breath, aimed, but didn't shoot. She brought the bow back down again. Murmurs traveled through the spectators. They hadn't seen her unnerved before.

She scanned the grandstands, trying to regain her focus. Horatio's eyes fixed on her. He couldn't imagine the pressure she must be feeling. Then he noticed she had stopped scanning the audience, and was staring in his direction.

"Is she looking at me?" Horatio asked himself.

"What's a hedgehog doing here?" she wondered. "Where is he from?"

He raised a paw and waved timidly, not even sure

she would notice, but hoping it might give her some encouragement from afar. Something in that small shy wave seemed familiar to Leala, but she wasn't sure why.

Leala took a deep breath and faced the target. Her nose began to twitch. She lowered her bow back down again and rubbed her nose. Then she raised her bow, aimed, and fired. Bull's-eye! The crowd leapt to their feet. "We have our new champion!" yelled the announcer. "Leala the Hedgehog, champion of the 127th Annual Tournament of Archers."

Leala exulted quietly. She shook Tran's paw. Through his weariness, he smiled at her. "Any other year," he told her, "I think I would have won."

"I think you're right," said Leala. "No one has come that close to beating me this year. Thanks for making me earn it."

Chapter 15

Horatio and Leala

Leala stood at the top of the awards platform. Tran stood to her left, Meerstud to her right. Both Tran and Meerstud had received medallions for finishing in second and third places. Now the time had come to award Leala with the championship trophy.

A raccoon in a plaid jacket and plaid hat that didn't match spoke to the spectators. "On behalf of the Tournament of Archers' Organizing Committee, it is my pleasure to award the 127th Annual Tournament of Archers championship trophy to Leala, the hedgehog."

The crowd whooped and cheered, then settled down to listen to Leala. "Thank you," she said, as she received the trophy. "This is a great honor, and I'll carry this trophy back to my village with pride." The grandstand broke out into another round of applause. "I'd also like to thank my fellow archers, particularly Tran and Meerstud, for such a tough match." She nodded to them and they nodded back. Then she held the trophy high, and the whole grandstand stood on their feet—stomping, clapping, hooting, and hollering.

"What a deserving champion," Horatio thought. He could barely see anything anymore as the larger mammals dwarfed him. As the mammals gradually left the grandstand, Whisklet, Whimser, and Horatio waited.

Once the crowd began to clear out, Whisklet whispered, "Let's go meet her."

"No," said Horatio. "I don't think we need to do that."

"Come on, you've never met another hedgehog before. Now's your chance." They each grabbed an arm and pushed him along.

Leala had a crowd of animals around her, some congratulating her, some just wanting to be near her. But when she saw Horatio approaching with two hamsters holding the Emblems of Graysent, she stepped away from the crowd to meet him.

"Hello, I saw you in the grandstand," she said. "I saw you wave."

"My name's Horatio. These are my friends Whisklet and Whimser. And Mish and Mosh."

"Nice to meet you. Where are you from?" she asked Horatio.

"I live up north along the river."

"I didn't know there were hedgehogs there."

"There aren't. I'm the only one." Horatio smiled awkwardly. He took a deep breath. "I'm a Solety."

"Oh," she noticed his knapsack with *Horatio* in red curved letters, encircled with stars, and the one brighter star with an arrow shooting through it. She could see by the knapsack's size and style that it was made for him years ago, when he was much younger.

Horatio tried to read her face. "Why would she want to talk to a Solety?" he asked himself.

"How did you get there? Where you live, I mean."

"I'm not sure. Do you know if any hedgehogs left the village years ago?"

"I don't think so. I don't know anyone who'd want to leave."

"Well," Horatio shrugged, "it's a mystery." He didn't know what more to say. "Congratulations on winning the championship. You shot really well."

"Thanks. Are you an archer too?"

"I got this bow yesterday as a gift. From a flying squirrel."

"It's a nice one. I can tell from the wood it's not a hedgehog bow. Hedgehogs make their bows out of yew. The bow you have is made from oak. Do you know how to shoot?"

"Does he ever," interjected Whimser.

"Well, I've only shot it a couple of times."

"Would you like to shoot at a tournament target? Give it a try."

"No, I couldn't."

"Sure, there's hardly anyone here."

"Show her," whispered Whimser.

Horatio grinned. He had been hoping for another opportunity. He took an arrow out of his quiver, stepped to the yellow line, and set his bow. "Here goes." He didn't feel nervous at all. He pulled the bow back, readied, and fired. His arrow hit the bull's-eye straight center.

"Good for you!" Leala said. "How long have you been shooting?"

"Since yesterday."

"Since yesterday!" she laughed. "You must be kidding."

"Really, I didn't even know I could shoot until yesterday, when I was given this bow."

"It's a mystery," said Whisklet, echoing Horatio's words.

Leala folded her arms. Now she didn't know what to make of him. "You're full of mysteries."

Horatio's ears turned pink. "I'm just trying to find my friend. He's an otter named Rollic."

"Is he lost?"

Horatio knew she wouldn't believe this part either. "No, it's a long story."

"He was kidnapped," said Whimser.

"Kidnapped!"

"He was kidnapped by a beast named Scarretchen."

"Why would he kidnap him?"

"You see," said Horatio, "it seems my father took one

of Scarretchen's wishing stones. And Scarretchen found out Rollic was my friend. So he kidnapped him to get to me. We've set off to rescue him."

"I've heard of those wishing stones. The myth says they are someplace along the sea on the west side of the river. It's just a myth though, right?"

Horatio shook his head. "No, they're real. Scarretchen guards them."

"Who is this Scarretchen?"

"No one knows what kind of creature he is now. He can turn himself into any type of creature he wants."

"Well I do hope you can find your friend. Are those the Emblems of Graysent?" she asked Whisklet and Whimser.

"Yes," said Whisklet. "Friends of Graysent stand against injustice wherever they see it. Scarretchen shouldn't be allowed to get away with this."

"No, he shouldn't. I wish you all the best. Let me get your arrow for you."

"Oh, no," said Horatio. "Thank you. I'll go get it."

"We'll go together," she insisted. Whisklet and Whimser waited.

Horatio and Leala walked side by side. "Your otter is lucky to have a friend like you," she said.

"He's the only friend I've got. That is, until I met Whisklet and Whimser. I've lived by myself as long as I can remember."

"There are no other hedgehogs where you live?"

"No. You're the first hedgehog I've ever seen."

She broke out in laughter without meaning to and covered her mouth. "I'm sorry. Is that true? I'm the first hedgehog you've ever seen!" Horatio's ears turned bright pink. Leala stared at him in disbelief as they walked. "Who is this boy?" she asked herself. She had never met anyone like him. "You must come to our village, after you rescue your friend. Will you?"

Horatio beamed. "I'd like that. I can't imagine a whole village of hedgehogs."

Leala laughed again. "It's a special place. You should come."

They reached the target and both reached for the arrow at the same time. Their paws touched. They both blushed. "Sorry," Horatio told her.

She pulled the arrow out and put it in his quiver. "Some day we should practice together. You can compete against me."

"Oh, no," Horatio grinned shyly. "I'm not that good."

"Still, it would be fun."

"It would be," he said dreamily.

When they got back, Whisklet and Whimser had been joined by two of the muscular badgers who had been sitting at the table.

"My escorts," Leala told them. "It was good to meet you."

"Nice meeting *you*," Whisklet and Whimser replied. Mish and Mosh twirled their antennae.

"It was a pleasure meeting you, Horatio."

"Thank you. It was my pleasure." They shook paws and forgot to let go. They just stared at each other for a while.

"Oh," Leala released his paw. "Come visit us."

"I will," said Horatio.

"Stay safe."

"I will."

Chapter 16

Down the River

As the three small mammals hurried down to the river to get to their raft, Horatio felt like he was floating in a fog. His surroundings seemed a little blurry. His knapsack and quiver of arrows never felt so light. He had a little lope in his stride.

"I think our friend *is* smitten," said Whisklet.

Horatio turned toward them and was about to deny it. But the look on his face gave him away. He couldn't deny it. Nor, when he came to think about it, did he want to.

The raft was waiting for them just as the painted turtles had promised. Whisklet took out some of their pecan tart and gave it to the turtles.

"Thanks," they said and lumbered off.

They lifted the raft toward the river and set it part way into the water. Whisklet grabbed hold of the rudder to steer. Horatio sat down on the raft and held on. Whisklet's Emblem was tied securely under the flap of his knapsack, so it extended out on either side.

"Here we go," said Whimser. He used his Emblem staff to push the raft out into the water.

"We're floating!" Horatio exclaimed. The current was so calm. The ride was far more pleasant than Horatio had imagined. He didn't feel the least bit worried about falling off. "It's great to get off our feet," said Horatio.

"And not have to worry about flying into quicksand," added Whimser.

Though the current seemed calm, they could tell, watching the shoreline go by, that they were traveling far faster than they would have if they had been walking.

"If we're lucky, we should make it to the Great Blue Bog before nightfall," said Whisklet. "We'll camp there for the night."

Out on the water, they passed some painted turtles they had seen before. The turtles popped up their heads as they floated by. "Did you find your otter?" one turtle called out. Horatio shook his head.

They came upon a little bump in the current, and the raft lifted gently up. "Whoa," Horatio said. "That was neat."

"Hey, Whisklet," Whimser called out, "isn't this about where we crossed the river on the first raft we built?"

"Yeah, it looks like it is. I remember those trees on the shore."

They coasted peacefully along the river for a couple of

hours or more. Even when the current picked up a little, Whisklet easily used the rudder to steer them away from any rocks jutting the surface.

There was no real reason for Whimser to paddle, so he sat down next to Horatio.

"How far downriver have you gone on a raft?" Horatio asked Whimser.

"Not this far. We mainly just wanted to cross the river. To see what it would look like from the other side. And to show we could do it. How many small mammals do you know can say they've set foot on both sides of the river?"

"I didn't think it could be done."

Whimser honked, "It can. And we have!" A sudden gust of wind lifted Whimser's hat off his head. He snatched it back in midair. "Nearly lost it," he exhaled.

"It's getting a little stronger up ahead," said Whisklet. "Nothing we can't handle, though."

"The current's definitely picking up," said Horatio.

"I'm going to get the raft closer to shore," Whisklet assured him. "It's a little rough to be out in the middle of the river."

The raft hit a wave and flew above the current—both the raft and Horatio's heart thudded loudly as the raft landed back down on the water. Horatio dug his claws into the raft and turned fearfully to Whisklet. "It doesn't look like it's getting any calmer. I'm not sure we should stay on the river if it's like this."

"Whimser, come help," called Whisklet. Whimser jumped back up and pushed on the rudder along with Whisklet. "Got to get it closer to shore."

"We're coming to some whitewater," said Whimser.

"Come on!" shouted Whisklet. "Harder!"

But the river carried the raft along as if it were simply a piece of wood. They looked upstream to see if there was any break in the current. What should have been a wide expanse of river was now open sky.

"A waterfall!" shouted Whisklet. Whisklet and Whimser exerted everything they had on the rudder. "To shore! To shore!"

"Rock!" yelled Whimser.

They closed their eyes and braced themselves. The raft hit the rock, but stayed intact. A cold splash drenched them. For a moment, the rock held them in place. But they could feel the current tugging at the raft, pulling it away from the rock.

"Steer the raft against the rock," shouted Horatio above the roar of the current. "Keep the raft here for as long as you can. I have an idea." Whisklet and Whimser pressed hard on the rudder.

Horatio now kneeled on the raft and took out the long rope from inside his knapsack. It came out nice and smooth, no tangles this time. He fastened one end of the rope tightly to an arrow, the other end to one of the sticks of the raft. "Okay. Whimser, push the raft from the rock! Toward the shore!" he yelled out.

Mish hid inside Whimser's knapsack, Mosh inside Horatio's.

The river loosened the raft from the rock. Whimser ran over and used his staff to push hard off the rock. Then he darted back to the rudder to help Whisklet steer. The raft hit a current that carried it tantalizingly close to the shore, but not close enough for them to jump off.

"Get down and grab hold of the raft!" Horatio yelled to them. He stood up and readied to fire. He crouched low with his feet spread apart to balance himself. The hamsters fell on their stomachs holding on for dear life.

The trees along the shore rushed by Horatio in a blur. The raft swayed up and down. He couldn't steady his shot. He picked out a solid, sturdy tree at the edge of the riverbank. He aimed his arrow for the middle of the tree's trunk and fired. His arrow stuck and held fast. The current continued to take the raft downward toward the edge. With a jolt the rope became taut and the raft came to a sudden halt, just above the waterfall. The jolt knocked Horatio off his feet, as the momentum of the current flung him down the raft. His arms flailed and he managed to grab hold of Whisklet's left foot. Whisklet reached down and grabbed hold of Horatio's knapsack.

"Unbelievable!" shouted Whimser. "You did it!"

"That's a shot legends are made of," said Whisklet pulling Horatio back up.

An immense sense of relief came over them, but vanished when they realized their lives depended on the rope holding. They looked at each other in terror.

"If this doesn't hold," Whisklet said, "we're dead. We have to get off the raft. The only way is to crawl along the rope."

None of them wanted to leave the fragile safety of the raft.

"Does anyone want to go first?" asked Whisklet.

"What happens if one of us tries to crawl along the rope and snaps it?" asked Whimser.

No one answered.

"We can't stay here!" shouted Whisklet. The raft let out a moan. "I'll go first if no one else wants to."

The rope was angled up toward the tree, just above the water.

"Will the rope stay above the water when we put our weight on it?" asked Whimser.

No one knew for sure. Whisklet grabbed hold of the rope, with all four paws. He made certain not to slice the rope with a claw. The rope dipped only a little. He crawled forward on top of the rope, keeping the rope between him and the river. The Emblem under the flap of his knapsack acted as a kind of ballast to keep him balanced. As he took a step the rope swayed a bit.

"Hold on!" cried Whimser. "Careful!"

Whisklet crawled a little farther. "It's holding," he called behind him.

The raft let out another low moaning creak. "Horatio, you go next," said Whimser, as he hurriedly secured his staff and his hat under the flap of his knapsack.

"Are you sure?"

"Yes, go ahead. Just be careful."

Horatio bent down and grabbed hold of the rope. The rope near the raft was wet and cold. He carefully stepped onto it, crawling on all fours like Whisklet. Beneath the rope he could see the fierce rush of the current. Each time Whisklet took a step, the rope swayed and Horatio had to quickly grab hold again. He knew if he tried to step when Whisklet was in mid-stride, while the rope was swaying, he might lose his balance altogether.

"Come on!" Horatio called back to Whimser. "The rope's holding steady."

"No, you keep going. I'll wait here until you both get to shore. The rope won't hold us all."

"Yes, it will," shouted Whisklet. "Come on! The raft's going to break off."

"Just keep going. I'm okay. You two get to shore first."

"I couldn't be so brave," thought Horatio.

The wind picked up. Whisklet and Horatio held on with all their might.

"We have to let the wind die down," cried Whisklet. "Then we need to move together. Otherwise we'll knock each other off when we shake the rope."

The wind settled down. "Left front paw," Whisklet called out. Whisklet and Horatio moved their left front paws. "Right front paw," he called again. "Left front paw, right front paw." Their pace picked up as they moved together. "That's right! That's better!" The raft let out a low moaning groan. "Whimser, climb on. Hurry! "

"No! You two get to shore."

"Faster!" Whisklet called to Horatio. All of a sudden one of the threads of the rope in front of Whisklet came loose. He froze. "The rope's fraying! Whimser, get on!" Whimser wouldn't move. "Come on, Horatio," Whisklet shouted. "Left, right, left, right," he barked. Whisklet carefully stepped over the frayed part to avoid snapping the rope. "Left, right, left, right," he continued.

Then Horatio slipped.

"Horatio!" Whimser cried.

Horatio hung upside down, his back to the river, the water lapping his knapsack. "It's freezing in here," Mosh cried. "But jusht don't let go."

It made Horatio dizzy to look at the shore, and see the trees upside down, with the river perilously close to sweeping him away. He fixed his eyes on the rope.

"Are you okay?" Whisklet called back.

"I'm holding," Horatio yelled to him. "Let's keep going."

"Left, right, left, right," Whisklet directed again, as Horatio traversed the rope upside down.

Whisklet could now see the riverbank beneath his paws. "I'm dropping off to the shore. The rope will spring back. Hold on really tight!"

Whisklet dropped off only to watch in dismay as the rope vibrated Horatio back and forth. The weight of the raft strained the rope even more. "Hold on!" he cried over the river. The raft let out another cracking moan. "Whimser, get on now! The rope will hold the two of you."

Whimser shook his head. "Let Horatio get to shore first," he called back.

Horatio shimmied onward as fast as he could go. He reached shore and fell on his back, landing with a thump on his knapsack. He heard a small "oof" from Mosh. "Sorry about that," Horatio told him.

"Okay, come on now, Whimser. Hurry!" Whisklet called out to his brother. Whimser didn't budge. "What are you doing?" Whimser shook his head. He was too terrified to move. "Whimser!" Whisklet shouted to him. "*Please!* You're going to die if you don't get off the raft."

"I can't!"

Whisklet stomped his foot, "Yes, you can. Come on! You've got to!"

The raft let out the loudest and lowest moan yet. It could give way at any moment. Whimser leaned forward and grabbed the rope. The raging river paralyzed him in fear.

"You can do it!"

He took the rope in all four paws. He looked away from the water and stared straight at Whisklet and Horatio.

"That's right. Come on, now." Whisklet grasped the rope near the arrow by the tree. "I've got the rope," he called out. "If the raft breaks, just hold on to the rope. I can drag you in." Whisklet knew he had no control of whether the arrow would hold.

Whimser shimmied a little farther toward them. The Emblem across his knapsack acted as ballast helping him stay balanced as it had for Whisklet. Whimser was completely off the raft now.

"You see, you can do it," Whisklet yelled to him.

Then the rope behind Whimser snapped, sending the raft plummeting down the waterfall and Whimser into the water. Whisklet pulled frantically. Horatio rushed to help. They pulled as fast and hard as they could.

"Did he hold on?" asked Horatio.

"I'm not sure."

Finally, Whimser's face appeared above the water, and he gasped and sputtered, as they pulled him up to the shore.

He collapsed on his back and Whisklet pressed his chest. Whimser coughed up the water he'd swallowed. Then he started to laugh out of sheer relief. "Honkle, Honkle," his nose was clogged.

"You darn fool," Whisklet scolded, then hugged him.

Horatio laughed. "We made it! All of us!" They shook paws and slapped each other on the back. The ground never felt so good under their feet.

Muffled sputtering sounds came from Whimser's knapsack. "Mish!" they cried. Whisklet and Horatio quickly grabbed Whimser's knapsack and pulled out a soggy and irritable Mish. "Shure, forget about me, will you. I should shlime you all when you shleep tonight."

Whimser's fur kept him warm, but both Mish and Mosh were shivering. Whisklet and Horatio untied their bandanas from their necks and put one over each snail. "Thanks," they said. Then Horatio took out the last soggy remains of the pecan tart from his knapsack. He gave them each a big chunk, which they ate with relish.

Whimser found his snake charmer. He drained it of water and tried it out. "It still works!" he said.

Whisklet just shook his head and smiled at him. The snake charmer never sounded better.

"Thanks for holding on to that rope," Whimser told him.

"As long as I had an arm to hold it with, I wasn't going to let go."

Horatio pulled out his arrow from the tree trunk. He untied the rope from the arrow, placed the rope back in his knapsack, and the arrow back in his quiver. He listened to the sound of the river inside him, Rollic's call. It was louder, more anxious than it had ever been. "It's okay," he whispered back. "We made it. We're okay. We're coming for you."

"I wouldn't have believed a shot like that, if I hadn't seen it with my own eyes," said Whimser, squeezing the water out of his hat one more time. "How'd you do it?"

"I don't know. Sometimes I feel my aim is so true—I can't miss."

A turtle swam up to them. The same turtle they had seen before. "What happened to your raft?"

"It went over the waterfall."

"I thought you knew about that."

"It's not even on the map!" yelled Whisklet.

"It's not as big as the first waterfall. Big enough to drown small mammals who can't swim," the turtle said as if mocking them. "Maybe not big enough to be drawn on a map, though. I thought you'd pull your raft to shore before the waterfall, and carry it down the riverbank—on the *other side* of the river."

"Why the other side?" asked Whisklet.

"Because that's Screech Forest behind you."

"Is that bad?"

The turtle's head bobbed, "It's haunted."

Chapter 17

Ghosts in Screech Forest

The day seemed to darken as soon as they entered Screech Forest. Long mossy threads hung from the branches of the trees. Their feet squished into the ground as if they were walking on sponges.

"This forest gives me the creeps," Whimser shuddered. Shapes seemed to fly past them.

"Bats," said Whisklet. "It's not even nighttime. What are they doing flying about at this time of day? What kind of forest is this?"

"They're usually harmless," Whimser said to Horatio. "But they fly all over the place to hunt for bugs." At that moment a bat swooped down right over their heads. "Worst of all—owls eat bats, and owls eat mammals like us. I don't know whether the owls here will respect the

Emblems of Graysent." The small mammals stepped more carefully through the forest.

A tree lurched at Horatio. "Yikes!" Horatio jumped back. "That tree's alive! It almost grabbed me."

They stared at the tree, waiting to see if it would move again, their legs shaking.

"I don't see anything," said Whimser. "Maybe it was just the wind."

"That wasn't the wind," insisted Horatio.

They stepped further on, slowly, huddled closer together. Another tree lurched at them. The three mammals jumped back. "They *are* alive!" Then another tree tried to grab them. "We're surrounded. Let's get out of here!" They tried to make a run for it but Horatio couldn't move his right leg.

"My leg's stuck on something," yelled Horatio. "I don't know what it is."

"My knapsack weighs a ton," yelled Whisklet. "I can't move."

"Mine too," yelled Whimser. He put one knee on the ground to support himself.

"I'm being shmushed," cried out Mish, who had been riding on top of Whimser's knapsack.

A large bat flew down and landed on a branch in front of them, hanging upside down and staring at them with a large toothy grin. "You can't see them," explained the bat.

"See who?"

"The ghosts," he grinned, revealing his sharp teeth.

"Bats are one of the few animals who can see ghosts. That's what makes us so spoooooky." His chest heaved as he chuckled at his own joke. "One is holding on to your leg," he said, pointing to Horatio with his wing. "And they're sitting on your knapsacks," he said, pointing to Whisklet and Whimser. "And some over there are hanging on to the branches of the trees." The trees seemed to jump out again. The three small mammals raised their paws over their heads. "Looks real, doesn't it."

"Tell them to go away and leave us alone," said Whisklet.

"They won't listen to me. They'll listen to the owls, but the owls are hungry at this time of day."

"We're under the protection of Graysent the Owl," shouted Whisklet, stomping his staff on the ground.

The bat noticed the hamsters' staffs, and his expression turned serious for the first time. "Then you can call the owls, but I'm not going to hang around. Wouldn't want an owl showing up and eating *me*," he flashed his spiky teeth again and flew off.

Whisklet became furious. Fighting an invisible foe made his blood boil. "We're under the protection of Graysent the Owl," he yelled at the top of his lungs over and over. But the ghosts wouldn't let go.

Another bat flew by. "You're not going to shout them away," he said as he disappeared back into the darkness.

Whisklet yelled again as loud as he could, "We're under the protection of Graysent the Owl."

Finally, a large screech owl landed in front of them, then another, then several more, encircling the small mammals. The owls were enormous, with grayish-white scraggly feathers, and tufts like horns on the tops of their heads. They were unlike any owls they had seen before.

The three small mammals tried to remain calm. They didn't know whether they were about to be eaten or freed. With all the courage he could muster, and trying to contain the fear in his voice, Whisklet stated again, "We're under the protection of Graysent the Owl." He raised the

Emblem. The yellow eyes of the staff glowed in the dark. "These are the Emblems of Graysent. We are his friends."

One of the screech owls took two steps forward and looked at the staff. His face no longer had the expression of a hunter on it. His eyes softened.

He spread his wings up, held them, and lowered them quickly, letting out a loud bone-rattling "SCREECH!" The small mammals nearly jumped out of their skins. But instantly the ghosts fled.

Horatio was able to move his leg. Whisklet and Whimser felt the weight released from their knapsacks. Mish could breathe normally again.

"What brings you to our forest?"

"We've set off to rescue an otter. We've been traveling downriver to get to the Great Blue Bog."

"Follow me. I'll show you the way out. This is not a forest for small mammals like you."

The owl escorted them through the forest, lifting his legs up high and somewhat awkwardly as he walked. It was clear the owl was unaccustomed to tramping through the woods on foot. The land began to slope sharply downward, and several times the incline made the three small mammals stumble. They grabbed hold of the mossy threads on the branches of the trees to keep from falling. They hadn't forgotten that moments ago the tree branches seemed to be grabbing at *them*.

Finally, the ground leveled off, and the owl turned toward the rush of water they heard through the trees.

Out of the woods, the sunlight reappeared. When they reached the river, they could see the waterfall that nearly cost them their lives. It was not a large waterfall, they had to admit, but the current fell over jagged boulders.

"Look!" cried Whimser. There, at the bottom of the boulders—as if it had been told to wait for them—lay their raft, beat up but not destroyed. It floated on the gentle pool of water just beyond where the waterfall rejoined the river. The bit of rope connected to the raft had gotten caught between two boulders, which had kept the raft from floating away altogether. "It doesn't look like it's in that bad of shape."

"Have you flown along the river to the sea?" Whisklet asked the owl.

"Yes, many times."

"Are there any more waterfalls or fast currents between here and the sea?"

"No, that is the last one," said the owl. "The currents are smooth from here on, even for small mammals on a raft."

"Maybe it's an omen," said Whisklet. "That we weren't supposed to lose our raft so soon after all." Whisklet looked at his traveling companions. "How do you feel? Are you willing to get back on the raft? I'd steer it so we stay near the shore."

"I am," said Horatio. Horatio knew it didn't make sense, but a part of him felt they owed it to the raft for having survived the fall—as if the raft deserved a second chance.

All eyes turned to Whimser now. "Okay, I'm game,"

said Whimser. "But let's keep to the shore."

"All right, then. Let's get this raft back into shape. Can you help us retrieve it?" Whisklet asked the owl.

The owl flew out to the raft, grasped the rope in his beak and flew back. The raft seemed tiny in the owl's immense wingspan.

The ivy needed to be tightened up again, but soon the raft was seaworthy.

"Farewell, friends of Graysent," the owl called to them, as they pushed off from shore once more.

Sure enough, the current remained calm and peaceful. They passed some smooth, sandy stretches along the riverbank, and wistfully imagined what it might be like to relax and lay in the sun.

Whisklet rested the side of his face against the rudder. He barely needed to steer. Horatio and Whimser sat back-to-back, knapsack against knapsack, to prop themselves up, and took a nap. Mish and Mosh dozed off too. They were all exhausted.

Toward dusk they saw a sign leaning against an embankment; it read, "Great Blue Bog." Whisklet brought the raft to shore, and they tied it to a tree.

"Let's camp here for tonight," said Whisklet. "We need a good night's rest. We'll head off to find Francis Hopper in the morning."

Whimser took off his knapsack, as if it were full of lead. "I wonder how he managed to escape Scarretchen."

"With any luck, we'll find out tomorrow," said

Whisklet. He opened his knapsack. "These are the last of our mom's biscuits." He shared them around. He gave Mish and Mosh a whole biscuit each this time.

Everyone waited. No one took a bite, not even the snails. "I know this is the last of the food our mom gave us, but she would have wanted us to eat it," Whisklet said.

As the three small mammals licked the final bits of biscuits off their paws, it began to dawn on them how far away from home they really were.

Chapter 18

Francis Hopper

The next morning the gang set off to find Francis Hopper. The embankment on this side of the river was steep, and they had to dig hard with their legs to make their way over it. A huge expanse of wetlands stretched out before them, spotted with dozens of great blue herons hunting for fish. They were certainly the biggest birds they had ever seen.

"So that's why it's called the Great Blue Bog," said Whisklet.

The herons stood like statues, but the intensity of their eyes, the tension in their bodies, and the curve of their necks, held taut in a crouching position, ready to strike at a fish, emanated a pulse of life no statue could possess.

"How will we ever find the right bullfrog in this huge bog?" whispered Whimser. The notion of interrupting a heron's hunt to ask for help seemed rude, even risky.

Much of the bog was underwater, teeming with vegetation so dark and green that they couldn't gauge its depth. Whimser took one step and fell in chest high, making a loud plunk. He stood there irritated at himself. Whisklet and Horatio, standing above him on a small piece of dry land, caught a glimpse of a circular shadow floating toward him. They reached in quickly to pull Whimser out. "A snapping turtle," said Whisklet.

"Really?" said Whimser, his heart pounding.

Horatio took out an arrow from his quiver, and readied his bow. He stood in front of the hamsters peering through the water. Just as quickly as it appeared, the circular shadow swam the other way.

"We won't make it through this bog on foot," said Whisklet. "We're going to need the raft." They trudged their way back, discouraged at the thought of how long it would take them to pull the raft up the steep embankment. They untied the raft from the tree, and tried to haul it up using the rope. It got stuck right below the top of the embankment. They couldn't pull it up over the embankment, nor could they set it back down, without the weight of the raft pulling them all the way down with it.

"Mish and Mosh," Whisklet called down to the snails standing on the shore. "Slime the raft as much as you can,

so that it slides easier." The three mammals held tight to the rope as Mish and Mosh went to work.

"Ready," Mish and Mosh called back, after they had covered the underbelly of the raft with slime.

With one hard yank, they finally got the raft unstuck and managed to pull it up onto level ground.

The raft floated easily atop the shallow waters of the bog. They knew a hungry snapping turtle could break through the bottom of the raft to get to them. But they hoped the turtles wouldn't notice the three meaty portions sitting on top of it.

They used their staffs to paddle through the water. The Emblems of Graysent seemed to have a magnetic effect on the herons. Each heron's head slowly, almost mechanically, turned toward them as they passed. Traveling into the depths of the bog, the blaring chirps, hums, and croaks of a thousand frogs, crickets, and katydids resounded from every direction. The jarring noise made the herons' silent stares even more unnerving.

One heron called out to them, "Are you here on behalf of Graysent the Owl?"

"Yes," replied Whisklet. "We're here to see Francis Hopper."

The heron answered, "I can take you to him."

"You speak in the language of mammals," said Whisklet. He did not know any birds, other than owls, who could speak to mammals. In the past, they relied on Mish and Mosh to translate for them.

"Yes, Francis Hopper taught us."

"How does a bullfrog know the language of mammals?" Whisklet whispered to Whimser, but he didn't want to pry into the matter any further.

The heron's strides were so long the small mammals had to paddle hard to keep up with him. The other herons' stares remained fixed on them, as they floated by. Eventually, they reached the end of the watery portion of the bog, and came to a dryer section near a woods.

"There's a trail that leads through the woods and arrives at a small stream. You will find him at the end of the stream."

"Thank you," Whisklet said.

They left their raft on the dry ground, untied, as there was no risk of it floating away here. Then they followed the trail till they reached the stream.

Suddenly, two great blue herons came out of the woods, lowering their heads all the way down in front of the small mammals' faces. "Who," they asked, "are you?"

"We are friends of Graysent," Whisklet said. "Graysent asked us to meet with Francis Hopper."

"Follow us."

They hurried to keep up with the two herons; even though the herons lifted their long legs so infrequently, they seemed to be standing still most of the time.

"They are good friends—Graysent and Francis Hopper," said the first heron, on their left. "Both wise. Francis Hopper showed us herons how to live in peace. We were feuding all the time, haggling with one another. But Francis Hopper taught us to be at bliss with our fish."

"How true," said the second heron, on their right. "The wise Francis Hopper."

"The wise and honorable Francis Hopper," corrected the first.

"The noble, wise, and honorable Francis Hopper," said the second heron, as they eyed each other.

They stopped and fell silent. They had arrived at the end of the stream where it created a small pool. Sitting atop a perfectly spherical rock, at the edge of the pool, sat a plump, tranquil bullfrog. His eyes were closed, a smile fixed across his face. The chirps and croaks of the bog had become a rhythmic drone in the distance.

The herons positioned themselves on either side of Francis Hopper. The three mammals and two snails waited. Francis Hopper kept his eyes closed.

"The honorable Francis Hopper is in meditation," whispered the heron standing to the bullfrog's right.

Francis Hopper's eyes finally opened a sliver. "Welcome friends of Graysent," he said as if expecting

them. "How is my old owl friend?"

"He's well, sir," said Whisklet, feeling instinctively that any friend of Graysent should be addressed as sir.

"What brings you to our bog?"

"An otter friend of ours has fallen under the spell of Scarretchen, and we need to rescue him. Graysent instructed us to come see you." They went on to explain everything. How Horatio kept hearing the sound of the river in Rollic's call. How they believed Horatio's father took one of Scarretchen's wishing stones.

"I see," Francis Hopper said, and the serene expression on his face hardened. "And you would like my advice?"

"Yes, sir."

"I am the only known creature to have seen Scarretchen, and lived to tell about it."

"How brave," said the heron on Francis Hopper's right.

"How brave and *strong*," said the heron on his left.

"Please, sit. I will tell you my story." The three mammals sat on rocks at the feet of Francis Hopper. "I will first tell you how I became a bullfrog. I used to be a human." The small mammals' eyes grew wide. They had never talked to a human before, or to a creature that had once been human. Francis Hopper read their faces. "Yes, if you would like to know what it's like to be human, I can tell you. Not very different from being a frog. The food is different of course. At any rate, I was a simple furniture maker. I learned about the wishing stones from an old map that described them, a map I actually found in a desk that once belonged to Scarretchen. A desk I made for him. Inside a hidden drawer that only Scarretchen and I knew existed. With map in hand, I traveled to the beach full of stones, and found a wishing stone. I wished my name would be known in all the lands. Instantly, I turned into a bullfrog. Of course, I had no idea that could happen. Nor did I have any desire to be anything but a man. I desperately tried to find another wishing stone. That's when Scarretchen came out of his lair.

"He knew I had used one of his wishing stones. He knew what I had wished for. He has given himself the power to hear every wish any creature makes with a wishing stone. Why he chose that power, I don't know. Perhaps some perverse desire to hear the wishes of vain misguided creatures.

"When he saw me as a bullfrog, he just pointed at me and laughed—a hideous, hateful laugh. He said I was a fool for thinking my wish would come true. Then, knowing I was his captive audience, he began the long, sordid tale of what happened to him when he used the wishing stones. That's when I realized who he was. He had been the master of the castle, for whom I made the desk. He hadn't died with the rest of the crew, as we thought, when his ship sank on the return trip of that fateful last voyage.

"All the while he told me his tale, I could feel the cool slime ooze from my body, my heart pounding against the thin membrane of my chest, as the desperation in me grew. I listened, hoping against hope he might find it in himself to turn me back into a man. But he wouldn't. He said I deserved my fate. 'Plenty of animals would love to dine on a plump bullfrog like you. Welcome to the world of the *hunted*,' he spitted out the last word.

"Then he saw the map lying on the stones, and accused me of stealing it from him. He crumpled it up and threw it into the sea. I told him I didn't steal it. That it was in his desk. And that after his wife's second husband died she gave me his desk—the desk I made for him years ago.

"He said, 'She is no longer married?'

"I told him, 'Now that she has lost two husbands, she has sworn she'll never marry again.'

"'And my boy has no father,' he said almost to himself.

"Then he let out a scream and gave me a kick with his boot. Fortunately, the kick didn't land solidly, and I was able to jump away from it. Naturally, I had to flee. I had no other choice.

"After days on the run, or on the hop, I found myself here. I was sure I would die a painful death as some animal devoured me for its dinner. But I realized I could communicate with animals, which I could never do as a human. I became a sort of sage to them, solving their problems, offering them advice and counsel. For even though I have the body of a bullfrog, I have the mind and lifespan of a man. They respected my opinions far too much to eat me.

"That is how I survived. By spreading peace and

tranquility. I *am* known throughout the lands, respected by creatures large and small. So my wish did come true—just not the way I expected it to. I have a plentiful supply of food, and a cool stream in which to swim. In short, I have everything I need. I am more content as a frog than I ever was as a man."

The three small mammals sat there stunned. Horatio finally spoke. "Sir, could you tell us, please, what's the best way for us to rescue Rollic?"

"Ahh, yes. You'll have to keep your wits about you. Scarretchen has probably turned your friend into some pathetic little creature and added it to his collection. If you can recognize your friend, and say his name out loud, he'll turn back into the otter you know.

"Or you could try to find your own wishing stone, and make a wish to bring Rollic back. But it's not easy to find such a stone. You must find the stone that is right for you. It may not be the same for every creature. One creature's wishing stone may be worthless to another. That's what happened to me—the stone that granted me a wish as a man was just a plain big rock to me when I became a bullfrog."

"Can a wishing stone grant more than one wish?" asked Horatio.

"Yes, it can—although usually not for the same creature. When a stone grants you a wish, it changes you—and you may no longer be right for the stone or the stone may no longer be right for you. You can tell if a stone will give you wishing powers because it becomes warm in your paw when you hold it. Not hot like an ember. But warm like a living thing. You can feel the energy inside it.

"But there's another risk you face if you use a wishing stone. And that is what might happen to you once you make a wish. For every time a wishing stone grants you a wish, it takes something away from you too. Look what happened to me. So you must be very careful what you wish for—as they say. You must think every word through. If you use one word rather than another, you might change completely how your wish turns out.

"In some ways, the wishing stones are as dangerous as poison, or even more so, because they are so enticing. Countless creatures have suffered after they made a wish with the wishing stones. Including Scarretchen. He became who he is because of the wishing stones."

"Yes, Graysent told us what happened to him," said Whisklet.

"Then you know. When I saw him he had the body of a man, with a long snout and razor-sharp teeth. His eyes glared bright green and his ears were black as coal. Instead of fingers, he had long, thick claws, sharper than any animal I've seen.

"But I believe he's become a creature the wishing stones can't even recognize now, that the wishing stones no longer work for him anymore. When I was fleeing from him, I heard him yelling to himself, 'If I only had one more wish.' Still he guards the stones, as if they were his own precious jewels.

"You must understand who you're dealing with. He has no conscience anymore; he has no sense of compassion or fairness. He's a sick, cruel, brutal creature, neither man nor animal. He could enslave you, torture you, kill you—whatever strikes his fancy at any given moment."

Francis Hopper suddenly snapped his tongue and snagged a green fly that buzzed by. The three small mammals jumped. "And it could happen that fast," he said, licking up some fly juice from his lower lip. "Steel yourselves, little ones. Steel yourselves."

Chapter 19

Leala's Discovery

Leala returned triumphantly to her village the same afternoon the three small mammals left Francis Hopper. She had returned on the Grand Wagon with her badger escorts. The badgers had taken turns and traveled all through the night to get her back to her home. Her village on the sea was their last stop.

One small hedgehog saw her coming and spread the news. The whole village came out to greet her—except for Aunt Quillity, who had been ill, and needed to stay in bed. They made way for her parents to be the first to meet her.

She raised the trophy over her head. A loud cheer went up.

"Well done!" her father exclaimed, as he helped her off the wagon. Then he thanked the badgers.

"Congratulations!" her mother gave her a hug.

Everyone gathered around the Grand Wagon for a while, shaking Leala's paw, until the badgers had to head back.

They had planned a big celebration for her, whether she had won or lost. They moved to the village social hall, a large burrow under the ground, safe from any predators. There was music, dancing, and food galore: carrot cake, apple pie, another scrumptious blackberry cobbler Leala's mom had made, and a table full of tarts.

She recounted the tournament over and over again in great detail. How she had to shoot 21 straight bull's-eyes to beat Tran. But she didn't speak about Horatio. She didn't want to be questioned about that. She knew what people might say, especially her father—"You met a *boy* hedgehog? A *boy*? Who is this *boy*?"

Toward the end of the evening, they began a ceremony Leala had seen several times over the years. Uncle Finneus opened up an ancient volume, *The Book of Archers*, which he kept in the rare books section of their library. He handed her a quill pen.

"One of the great honors in our village is to be added to *The Book of Archers*. Now it's Leala's turn." He then opened the large volume, and carefully turned the aged pages to the appropriate place.

Her name would be listed as a champion archer,

beside some of the greatest hedgehog archers of all time. She scanned their signatures: Surefire, Spiker Thorn, the Great Yvonne, some dating back hundreds of years. Then she signed below theirs—Leala the Archer.

The ceremony was too steeped in tradition for applause, but the honor in the silence moved Leala even more.

"This is where your trophy will go," Uncle Finneus whispered to Leala, showing her a spot in a display case with the label, Leala the Archer. The case was full of medallions and trophies of years past. "But before we place your trophy here, there's someone who hasn't seen it yet, who would very much like to."

"Aunt Quillity!" said Leala.

"Could you take your trophy to her? It would make her feel so much better."

"Of course. I'll go right now."

Leala traveled underground from the social hall through winding passages to Aunt Qullity's burrow. She knocked on the door. "Come in," she heard.

Aunt Quillity was lying in bed looking at an old picture album. She closed it as Leala entered the room. "Look at you!" she brightened up at seeing Leala. "You won!"

"I did! How are you feeling?"

"Much better now that you've arrived. Tell me everything. What was it like?"

Leala recounted the tournament once more. "I started to get nervous during the championship round, since it was just Tran and me. He looked like he would never miss. But I stayed focused, the way Dad taught me. I didn't let anything distract me—even when my nose twitched."

Aunt Quillity laughed. Then she looked down at her picture album and sighed, "Every year, at this time, it reminds me of my sons. My youngest son was gifted in archery too. The first time he picked up a bow and arrow, the very first time, he hit the bull's-eye. He was only about three years old at the time. No one had seen anything like it. He didn't need any training or instruction. It was just a natural gift. I bet he would have competed in the Tournament of Archers if he had grown up. I've been looking at some of their pictures in my album. I don't think you've ever seen these. Would you like to?"

"Sure," said Leala. Aunt Quillity rarely spoke about her two sons to Leala, and Leala never felt comfortable asking about them. Leala had been told they were killed by hawks, years ago, when both boys were little. The village saw the attack on her oldest son. Only a few weeks later, her youngest one apparently wandered off on his own, as young hedgehogs sometimes do, and was never seen again.

Aunt Quillity opened the large picture album, and turned the pages. "Here, this is my youngest. The last picture we have of him. He liked to wave his paw when he was having his picture made."

"I have this vague memory of him waving to me," said Leala.

"You may remember him a little. He was about four years old when he was taken from us. You were a year younger than him. Now this is another picture made a few days earlier, while we were foraging in the woods. I knitted that knapsack for him. He took it everywhere. He was so proud of it."

Leala looked closely at the picture. On the top flap of the knapsack was the name *Horatio* in curving red letters, encircled with stars, and one star at the top with an arrow shooting through it.

Her mouth fell open. "I've seen that knapsack!" she thought. "That's Horatio's knapsack!"

"I forgot your boy's name was Horatio," said Leala aloud, keeping her voice composed.

"That's right. Now this is a picture of my older son," Aunt Quillity continued.

"Aunt Quillity," Leala interrupted, "go back to the picture of Horatio. That's a beautiful knapsack."

"Thank you."

"Do you still have it?"

"No, unfortunately Horatio was wearing it when he was attacked. It was never found."

Leala's heart started pounding. "He was just foraging on his own that day? No one else was around?"

"That's right. I had told him not to go off on his own. But he was a strong-willed boy. Finneus was away at the time. Off on one of his exploring trips. Telling Finneus what had happened was heart wrenching."

"Where was he exploring?"

"He was going to explore a beach they say contains magical wishing stones. A myth of course. Still, he was always interested in exploring. Finding new things. But I'm sure Finneus felt Horatio might not have gone off on his own that day had he been here with him."

"Magical stones!" Leala said to herself. "Those are the stones Horatio was telling me about! He said his father took one. Could that be Uncle Finneus?" she wondered. "And he was a naturally gifted archer?" Leala asked Aunt Quillity.

"Yes, he might have been tough competition for you this year, if he were still here," Aunt Quillity chuckled.

"He might have been," Leala agreed. She remembered how surprised she was when Horatio had hit the bull's-eye on his first shot. "Is that design on the knapsack, was that a common design back then?"

"No, no. It was my design. I put the arrow through the top star as if to say to Horatio he should aim for the stars. He was only about three years old when I made this knapsack for him."

"Could it really be?" Leala wondered. Could the Horatio she met at the tournament be their son after all these years? How could that be possible? It seemed preposterous to her. "I need to talk to Uncle Finneus to know for sure," she told herself. "I don't want to say anything. It would be a cruel joke to say anything to anyone if I'm wrong."

"Aunt Quillity," she said. "I don't want to keep you up too late."

"Of course, dear. I'll see you tomorrow."

Leala returned to the social hall. Uncle Finneus was waiting for her along with the others. Leala handed him the trophy. He called for everyone's attention. "Leala the Archer," he said as he put the trophy in the display case. Everyone now applauded.

Leala beamed to those around her, but she could only think about Horatio. She waited patiently as Uncle Finneus and a few others gazed at the trophies in the display case. Finally, he was the only one there.

She came up to him quietly. "Uncle Finneus, did you ever go exploring for the wishing stones? The ones in the myth that lie across the sea?"

"Who told you that?"

"Aunt Quillity. She was showing me some old pictures."

"About Horatio?"

Leala nodded and suppressed a gulp.

"Did Aunt Quillity tell you how gifted Horatio was in archery? I've never seen anyone take to archery so fast."

"Yes, she did."

"Every year around the time of the Tournament, she likes to bring out the picture album. After my oldest son was killed, I didn't know what to do. I needed to get away. I found a map about a year earlier that had landed on the shore near here. The map showed the location of these wishing stones along the ocean on the other side of the river. So I followed the map. It was just a lark. I should never have left. The one I'm wearing around my neck is the stone I found there. I noticed it because it had a little hole inside it—just the right size to put a string through. I even made a wish with it. They say a wishing stone will become warm when you hold it, and this one did. I had the crazy notion it might be real. But it must have been warmed from the sun. Now when I hold it, it doesn't get warm. They're not real wishing stones.

"When I returned, Quillity told me what happened to Horatio. I've always blamed myself for being away. I've worn this stone ever since, in his memory. I found it the day Horatio was killed."

"What did you wish for?"

"Oh, it doesn't matter now. How I wish it had come true. But I've never gone back to that beach. I learned afterward a strange beast lives there. He's very dangerous. They say only one creature has seen the beast and survived to tell about it."

"That beast must be Scarretchen," Leala thought. "Uncle Finneus is wearing the wishing stone Scarretchen thinks he took from him. What if Horatio doesn't survive? If I tell Uncle Finneus and Aunt Quillity about Horatio and he doesn't live, it'd break their hearts all over again. I have to go find him. Tell him who his parents are. I have to bring him back—safe."

"Uncle Finneus," Leala asked, "How did you cross the river to get to the stones?"

"Well, I actually hitched a ride on a sea tortoise. Early in the morning, way before you wake up, the tortoises come in to rest on the shore. I asked one to give me a ride, and he did. They're very nice creatures. By the time the sun comes up, they've all gone back out to sea."

He stared into the display case again. "I always thought we'd put Horatio's trophy in this display case one day."

At the end of the evening, Leala returned with her parents to their burrow for the night. "I should go to bed. I'm really tired."

"We'll see you in the morning," they told her and gave her a hug.

Leala lay in her bed, staring up into the dark. Her heart kept racing. "I've got to catch up with Horatio. Before it's too late. At midnight tonight, I'm gone."

Around dusk the same night, the three small mammals and two snails reached the sea on their raft. They gaped open-mouthed at the ocean in front of them. Horatio had never imagined anything could make the river seem small, but the ocean seemed to go on forever.

They camped on the side of the river where the wishing stones lay. "We'll get up early in the morning before dawn," said Whisklet. "We'll take the raft along the shore to the stones. We have to be absolutely quiet when we land on the beach. And we have to move fast."

Chapter 20

To the Rescue

The three small mammals woke in the wee hours of the morning. The sky was still gray; the fog hung thick; the tide retreated as the sea swayed. They used the Emblems to paddle their raft quietly along the shore. Mish and Mosh rode atop the Emblems to keep away from the salt water—salt being deadly to snails.

"Hang on to the Emblemsh tight," whispered Mish.

"Don't worry, we will," Whimser whispered back.

They had all agreed to search for a wishing stone, and wish for Rollic's return. They had settled on the wording of their wish: "I wish for Rollic to return as an otter the way he was before Scarretchen captured him." They knew the risks of making a wish with these stones, but decided it was less dangerous than facing Scarretchen himself. If everything worked out, they would escape with Rollic, before Scarretchen knew what they were up to. Their plan depended on their landing on the beach in secrecy.

Finally, they reached the point on the shore where a deep inlet began. "This is it," whispered Whisklet. Within that inlet, covered in fog, lay the beach of wishing stones.

They paddled onward, slowly, into the fog. They listened to every dip of their Emblems into the water, every plop of water into the sea as they pulled the Emblems out.

As they reached the beach, the underbelly of the raft scraped against the stones. The noise made them cringe. They held their breath and listened. No sound came from the forest behind the beach. They had not given themselves away. Their feet splashed the water as they stepped off the raft. They stopped and listened again. Still, the forest remained silent.

For the first time, now they could see the stones clearly. They were perfectly polished and round. Each one shimmered like a gem. Horatio could see how a creature could fall in love with these stones, spend hours fondling them, growing heedless to the dangers.

Horatio remembered what Francis Hopper had told them—"a wishing stone becomes warm in your paw when you hold it."

"But how long do you need to hold it before it turns warm?" Horatio wondered.

The three small mammals picked up one stone after another, setting them back down carefully, making sure they didn't drop one stone against another. They knew at any moment Scarretchen could appear. Every time Horatio bent down to pick up a stone, he feared that as soon as he raised himself back up, Scarretchen would be standing there. Their fear clouded their thoughts as the fog clouded their vision. They stayed close together, so as not to lose sight of each other. Now and then they'd silently ask each other, "Any success?" But each time they received a shake of the head.

Whisklet instructed Mish and Mosh to climb to the top of a tall tree nearby. "You might not be able to see us through the fog, but you might be able to see if anything is coming through the woods. Whistle if you do." Mish and Mosh nodded, and disappeared in an instant.

A burnt-red rock caught Horatio's eye. There was nothing elegant about its shape. But the color was dark and bold. He picked it up, and it felt softer and smoother than the other rocks, almost as if it were made of clay. He loved the feel of it. He pressed it between both paws. He didn't feel it getting warm. But he didn't want to let it go.

A thunderous crack came from the forest—then another and another. Something heavy was stomping through the woods, moving swiftly, getting louder and closer. The snails' whistles echoed across the beach. They had seen it.

Whisklet and Whimser raised the Emblems high. Horatio tucked the rock in his pocket. He took an arrow from his quiver and readied his bow. His heart pounded so hard it pained him.

The shape of an enormous creature emerged through the fog. Scarretchen stood before them. He had the body of a man, but the head of a beast with a long snout and sharp teeth and fiery green eyes that bulged out of his face. Instead of hands he had paws, and his thick claws curved around a staff. He wore a long black coat, with a high collar that came up to his black leathery ears.

"I thought it might be you," he spoke quietly, as if he were making conversation. "Good. I knew it was only a matter of time. You've come to see what happened to your friend. What *was* his name—Rollic?" He turned around and walked back toward the woods.

They stood stunned. Were they really supposed to follow him? Was it a trap?

Whimser started grabbing stones frantically. "Stop," said Whisklet. "He's not going to tell us again. If we want to live, we need to follow him."

The three small mammals scurried after Scarretchen. He led them deeper into the woods. He did not slow down. Mish and Mosh caught up with them, and rode atop the knapsacks.

At times they could only keep track of Scarretchen by

the black shape of his coat moving through the trees. The forest was dense. The trees were tall, thin and bent; the branches crooked and spindly.

They followed the shape of the beast through the woods to the side of a hill.

"Where did he go?" Horatio whispered.

"This way," a voice called from an opening in the hill. The three small mammals stopped at the entrance of a cave.

"Rollic must be in there," Whisklet pointed to the entrance.

They ventured in. It was pitch-black inside. They stumbled and groped blindly at the walls. They only hoped they wouldn't fall into an abyss.

"Mish and Mosh, where are you?" asked Whimser.

"We're right in front of you," Mish whispered back. "We can shee fine. We're in the middle of a huge tunnel. It keepsh going and going."

"Okay, lead the way. But don't go too fast," Whimser told them.

"*This way,*" the voice commanded.

A stream of light entered the cave from above, and they found themselves inside a huge cavern. Tucked in the ledges and crevices of the cavern were scores of rusty cages and discolored jars. A few were illuminated. Most were in the damp, darkened portions of the cavern.

Scarretchen stepped beneath the light. "How do you like my collection?"

It was then that Horatio noticed a frail mouse in one of the cages. The light shined on him enough for Horatio to see him clearly. The mouse grasped the bars of his cage and pressed his small nose between the bars as he peered out at them. Tears fell on his cheeks.

Horatio saw a cracked jar on a ledge a few feet from him. He walked over to it. Inside a blind mole dug furiously at the dirt, as if trying to escape. Next to the mole were more jars. One contained a large toad covered in warts. He had one large red wart on each eyelid. Another jar contained a dung beetle, eating its meal. Above them sat more jars, and Horatio noticed a Wingwot inside one. She held her head in her cup-shaped hands, and sat miserably on a rock.

"That mole is the newest one in my collection—added her yesterday. She was a red fox coming to save her son. He's now a termite sitting in a jar somewhere. I gave her a chance. She could have picked him out. She guessed wrong. Now it's your turn. Pick out your friend. He's here. Say his name out loud, and he'll turn into the otter you know. If you guess right, he'll be free to go. Guess wrong, and there's an empty cage waiting for you—right there." Scarretchen pointed with his staff to a cage high on the cavern wall. "Any last requests?" Scarretchen's laugh seemed to make the whole cavern rumble.

"How can I tell which one is Rollic?" Horatio asked himself. Some of the jars and cages were so high up on the cavern walls; he didn't know how he could inspect them. The mouse reached out his paw, pleading for Horatio to pick him. "I'd like to free you. But I can't if you're not Rollic," Horatio told him.

"No talking," Scarretchen said calmly.

Horatio suspected Scarretchen had turned Rollic into some loathsome creature. The dung beetle seemed particularly disgusting to Horatio. "Rollic would hate to be that," he thought. "Maybe it would be okay if you were born a dung beetle," Horatio thought. "But to be turned into one?" He shuddered. The warty toad seemed to be a wretched creature too. "But are they Rollic?" None of the creatures on the lower portion of the cavern seemed like Rollic to Horatio.

Horatio needed to see the creatures in the cages higher up. He handed Whisklet his bow and quiver of arrows, but he kept his knapsack in case he needed the rope to repel himself down. He used the crevices within the walls to climb up the cavern. Slowly, painstakingly, Horatio worked his way up and down the cavern walls. He saw creatures he'd never seen before: a large black millipede, a stick bug, a scorpion. None of them seemed like Rollic, though.

On one small ledge high on the cavern wall, stood a tiny jar almost too small to notice. Horatio couldn't even see how he could reach it. Near the jar, he saw a large ledge, which held a cage. "I might be able to leap from the larger ledge to the smaller one," he thought. "But if I miss?" He left his question unanswered. He climbed up one crevice after another. He finally lifted himself onto the ledge with the cage. Inside the cage, a horned lizard flicked his tongue at Horatio. One of the lizard's toes rested in a small pool of water, filled with mosquitoes. "I don't think that's Rollic," Horatio said to himself.

Horatio stood at the far end of the larger ledge. "I need one good running jump." He ran and leapt, bumping into the jar on the smaller ledge, and grabbing hold of it just in time to prevent it from falling off. "Made it!"

Inside the jar was a tiny moth. It barely had room to fly. Its thin black legs pressed against the glass of the jar. Its beady black eyes stared straight at Horatio. It flapped its wings. "Is he trying to tell me something?" Horatio wondered. Horatio noticed the white tips on the moth's front legs. Other than the tips they were all black. His back legs were all black too. "Why are only the tips of your front legs white?" Horatio pressed his face to the jar. The moth flapped its wings again. "You're Rollic, aren't you?" The moth's black eyes seemed to grow bigger. "I know you," Horatio said out loud. "You're Rollic!"

In an instant Horatio found himself lying on the floor of the cavern with a furry otter over him, his white paws pressed to Horatio's chest. "Rollic!" Horatio cried.

"Horatio!" Rollic's furry body shook. His tail wagged. He licked the tip of Horatio's nose. "You saved me!"

Chapter 21

Horatio's One Wish

Whisklet and Whimser ran over to congratulate Horatio. "Well done!"

Mish and Mosh gave three cheerful whistles.

A cage came down on Horatio like a loud crack of fire. "Clever," Scarretchen held the cage to his face so that his green eyes seared right into Horatio.

"No!" cried Rollic.

"That's not fair!" shouted Whisklet. "He found Rollic. Let him go."

"I said *your friend* would be free to go," Scarretchen told Horatio as he rattled the cage, and Horatio was flung from side to side. "I didn't say *you* would. You came for

your friend. Now your father will come for you. Your father has one of my wishing stones—the only creature to escape with one. I would have gone after him, but he would have used the stone against me. He wears it around his neck everywhere he goes, flaunting it. I've seen him in your village. Disguised myself any number of times. But now I have you. He'll come to *me* now—with the wishing stone."

"He's seen my father?" thought Horatio. "That can't be. My father's been dead for seven years." Horatio grasped the bars of his cage. He shook the bars, but the lock on the cage was shut tight. He peered through the bars to see the keyhole of the lock.

"You'd like the key, wouldn't you?" Scarretchen held it in his clawed hand in front of Horatio. "Being trapped in the body of another animal is a cage with no key. What will it be? I think a roach would suit you."

Scarretchen pointed his staff at Horatio. Horatio covered his head with his paws. But to his amazement, nothing happened—he remained unchanged. Horatio could sense the rage inside Scarretchen. "So be it. You'll remain safe inside your cage," he laughed again, and Horatio's skin crawled listening to it. He placed Horatio's cage far away from the others, on a high ledge on a wall that was as smooth as glass.

Then Scarretchen turned to Whisklet and Whimser. "Go tell Horatio's father what has happened to him. Go to his village. Tell him to bring the wishing stone with him.

I want that stone!" Scarretchen stormed back down the tunnel, holding his staff high. "Get me that stone!" echoed over and over through the cavern.

"What are we going to do?" Horatio called down below. "He thinks my father's alive. But that can't be. Can it?"

"We'll go to your village. We'll find out about your father," said Whisklet. "We'll be back as soon as we can."

"Why wasn't he able to change me into some other animal?"

"He tried, but he couldn't for some reason."

"Don't worry, Horatio," Rollic called up to him. "You saved me. I'll save you. I promise. We'll get you out."

"Come on," they heard Mosh's voice call from the tunnel. "Follow ush."

Whisklet, Whimser, and Rollic dashed into the tunnel toward the entrance of the cave. The blackness brought them to a halt. They stumbled blindly.

"Keep going," Mish's voice called to them.

"I can't see a thing," said Whimser.

"Whimser?" a voiced whispered in the dark.

"Was that you, Mish?" Whimser asked.

"No, it washn't me."

"Where are you?" the voice said again.

"Someone else is in this tunnel," Whimser whispered to Whisklet.

"Hey!" they heard the snails call out ahead of them.

At that moment, a paw groping in the dark poked Whimser on the side of the face. "Yikes! Something's trying to grab me!"

"Whimser?" the voice whispered again.

"Get away from me!" Whimser shouted back.

"It's me, Leala."

"Leala!" Whisklet and Whimser exclaimed at once. None of them could see the others.

"What in the world are you doing here?" whispered Whisklet.

"I came to help. I followed you through the woods but didn't know where you went. Then I saw the entrance to the cave, and heard Scarretchen laughing. I hid in the tunnel. He stepped right over me when he ran out. Where's Horatio?"

"Scarretchen's trapped him in a cage. He wants us to go get Horatio's father."

"I know his father. He's Uncle Finneus. He lives in the village. That's why I came here. Horatio's been missing all these years. Take me to him."

"We'll show you." They took Leala to the cavern of prisoners.

"Leala!" Horatio cried. "What …"

"Shhh," she whispered. "I came to help you. Your parents live in the village. I know them. They thought you'd been killed."

"My parents *are* alive?"

"Yes!"

"Then I'm not a Solety!" His parents were out there, beyond the cavern walls, doing everyday things, alive and well. He could actually meet them, if he were free. If only he were free. Yet now he had no way of reaching them. A sharp pang of longing filled him. He peered out through the bars of the cage. "What am I to do?"

"Don't worry, we'll get you out."

"How did this happen? How did I ever get separated from them? How did I end up so far away?"

"They thought a hawk attacked you. Maybe a hawk carried you upriver and dropped you unharmed."

"How could that be? A hawk wouldn't carry its prey that far. It doesn't make sense."

"I know. None of this makes sense. All I know is your parents are alive in the village."

Horatio shook the bars of the cage as hard as he could. Then he limply let go. "I'm trapped in here."

The sun had grown stronger, and Horatio's cage was illuminated fully now.

"If we could only pick the lock," said Whisklet. "We need something long and thin."

"I have something long and thin," said Leala as she pulled out an arrow.

"Of course! But how are we going to reach the lock? There are no crevices anywhere on that wall."

"Maybe you can climb up using my rope," Horatio said. He took the rope from his knapsack, tied it to his cage, and threw it down. It wasn't nearly long enough to reach the cavern floor.

Whisklet and Whimser tried vainly to grab hold of the

rope. Even standing on each other's shoulders, it was too high off the ground. "It won't work," said Whisklet.

"I can reach his cage," said Leala, as she readied her bow and pulled back the arrow. "Horatio, get back and lay low," Leala called up to him. "I'm going to aim for the lock."

"You're going to try to hit the keyhole from down there?"

"Watch me!" She called back up. Then she paused. "No, don't watch. Better cover your head."

Horatio moved back to the far end of the cage, lay on his stomach, and placed his paws over his head.

The keyhole was much smaller than any bull's-eye Leala had ever aimed for. She readied her bow, aimed, and fired. The first arrow shot through the bars of the cage and bounced off the wall.

"Careful," Horatio called down to her, after the arrow nearly ricocheted into him.

Her next shot bounced off the lock.

"That was closer," said Whisklet.

She tried one arrow after another. Each time an arrow bounced off, Whisklet, Whimser, or Rollic retrieved it.

The other creatures in their cages stared intently at Leala. Their dull, dreary lives had become interesting for a moment.

Leala took one of the arrows from Horatio's quiver, which Whisklet had been holding for him. She pulled back her bow and held it taut—in her mind she saw the aged pages of *The Book of Archers*, and her signature underneath those of all the great archers of years past. She fired again. This time the arrow struck the keyhole dead center! With a loud click, the door of the cage creaked open.

"You did it!" Rollic cried.

"Wow!" Horatio exclaimed. He put his knapsack back on, stepped out of the cage carefully, and shimmied his way down the rope. He dangled on the end of the rope trying to decide whether it was too far to jump. "There's no other way," he said to himself. He let go and rolled when he landed. Then he bounced back up unscathed. He ran and gave Leala a hug. "Thank you! I don't know what I would have done!"

"Let's get out of here," said Whisklet. "Before Scarretchen gets back."

They started to work their way through the dark tunnel again. A familiar hissing sound came through the passageway. "Hold on!" whispered Whisklet.

"It's a snake," said Whimser.

"We'll be right back," said Mish. A few seconds passed before the snails rejoined the group in the cavern.

"It'sh a sherpent," said Mish. "Huge. About double the shize of that shnake we shaw in the field."

"He wasn't there when I entered the tunnel," said Leala.

"We talked to him," said Mish. "He guardsh the entrance of the cave only when Shcarretchen'sh away. He hash to shtay at the entrance. Shcarretchen told him he could eat one of the hamstersh on our way out but to let the other one go."

"Scarretchen is pure evil," said Whimser. "But he doesn't know about this—my secret weapon." Whimser took out the snake charmer and began to play. Mish and Mosh dashed down the tunnel to the serpent. The mammals waited for the snails' three whistles, their signal that the serpent had been hypnotized.

"What's taking so long," wondered Whisklet.

"Pssht," they heard Mish's voice through the darkness. "It'sh not working. Do you know any other shnake charm mushic?"

"I know one other tune, but not very well." Whimser's heart began to race.

"Try it. There'sh nothing elshe we can do."

"We've got to hurry," said Whisklet. "We've got to get past that serpent before Scarretchen comes back."

Whimser put the snake charmer to his mouth again. He was too nervous to make the notes come out right. They were painfully off-key.

"What the heck is that?" asked Whisklet. Everyone was covering their ears. Whimser tried again. The screeching sounds reverberated through the tunnel.

Mish had slimed back. "What are you doing?"

"Is it hypnotizing him?" asked Whimser.

"No, it'sh ticking him off. He can't shtand it."

"I'm sorry. I'm too jittery."

"Come on, Whimser," Whisklet tried to encourage

him, but he couldn't hide the frantic tone in his voice. "We're going to be trapped in here like the others."

Then Mosh returned. "He'sh not a real sherpent. Shcarretchen turned him into one. He ushed to be a shrew. That'sh why the shnake charmer ishn't working. He shaysh he'sh misherable. Shometimesh he hash to eat hish own kind."

"So he's really a small mammal too?" asked Whisklet. "Tell him we're carrying the Emblems of Graysent."

Mosh glided back to the serpent and then returned. "He can't believe Friendsh of Grayshent are here. He shaysh you're honored and can pash." The group raised their fists in a silent cheer.

"Thank goodness," whispered Rollic.

Horatio turned and looked back at all of the creatures along the cavern walls. "I was so close to being one of them. Trapped in the body of a roach." He stuck his hands in his pocket. He felt the red clay stone he had found. He had completely forgotten about it until now. His paw became very warm. He pulled the stone out. "I think this is a wishing stone," he whispered.

"What do you mean?" asked Whisklet.

"Where'd you get it?"

"At the beach. It feels like it's coming alive in my paw."

"Is it turning warm?"

Horatio nodded. "I want to make a wish."

"No, don't," said Whisklet. "You don't know what will happen. You're safe now. Rollic's safe. Let's get out of here."

"I can't leave all of these creatures like this."

"Horatio, don't. There's nothing you can do."

"I could make a wish."

"We need to get out of here before Scarretchen gets back. He may have heard the noise. Besides, every time the stones grant you a wish they take something away. You could turn into some other creature, the way Francis Hopper turned into a bullfrog."

"Not if my wish comes true. I can't just leave them. There could be two creatures in here that are best friends like Rollic and me. Remember Latch? His good friend's boy disappeared. Then his friend disappeared. They could be here."

Horatio closed his eyes and held the rock tight. "I wish for a world where all creatures can be who they were truly meant to be."

The whole cavern rocked. In a flash the cavern was full of creatures everywhere hugging, crying, and jumping for joy. Oh, what jubilation!

Two squirrels, a father and a son, embraced each other. "We're free! You're back."

A father mockingbird enveloped his daughter in his wings. "I thought I'd never see you again."

A mother red fox nuzzled her young son. "You're safe now."

Two brother muskrats hugged each other, "We're muskrats again, dude!" and slapped paws in high-fives.

"I've never seen anything like this!" shouted Whimser, as he gave a hop and clapped his hands.

"Your wish came true," cried Whisklet. "You did it!"

Horatio was too dumbfounded to speak. Scores and scores of animals, of all shapes and sizes, were paired up together, reunited at last: rabbits, woodpeckers, geese, mice, and moles.

Flying high up in the cavern, a solitary Wingwot hovered. It was the same Wingwot Horatio had seen in the jar. She flew down to Horatio. He put his paw out, and she landed on it. "Could you be Meerious?" he asked.

"I am. How'd you know?"

"I met Winfred."

"Oh my! How is my dear Winfred? I had no idea if he would still be alive."

"He's alive and well but misses you. I saw him on the big rock along the river."

"Thank you for rescuing me. For rescuing all of us."

"But Scarretchen didn't change you into some other creature. Why?"

"You can't cast a spell on a Wingwot. That's one of our

secrets. He simply trapped me in a jar."

"So he couldn't cast a spell on you to call to Winfred. The way Rollic called to me. That's why Winfred didn't come for you."

"That's right, and I'm glad for it. I wouldn't have wanted him to try to rescue me and end up trapped here too. I'm going to fly to the big rock right now. I've spent far too much time away."

"Good luck to you. Oh, can you tell the other Wingwots I found Rollic? He's safe. Perhaps one of them can tell his family. They live north of the rock. We're going to take Rollic to the hedgehog village with us."

"I certainly will. We'll spread the news. Every creature in every land will hear of what you did today, Horatio."

"It was just a simple wish."

"But perhaps the most important wish of all."

Meerious fluttered away and sped through the opening at the top of the cave; the light streaming on her as she flew made her yellow wings dance.

The father and son squirrels approached Horatio. The two held on to each other as if never wanting to let go. Horatio realized they were flying squirrels. "Could you be friends of Latch?" he asked.

"We are indeed. Do you know him?"

"He saved our lives from Globdum. He lent me this bow and arrows. It was his bow when he was a boy." Horatio offered it to them. "You can return it to him for me."

The father squirrel shook his head, "I remember when his father made that bow for him."

"It's meant a lot to me," Horatio said, looking fondly at the bow. "We wouldn't have survived our journey without it."

"Then hold on to it. I'm sure Latch is glad it's in good hands. You've saved *our* lives. I can't tell you how grateful we are."

One by one, each pair of animals came up to Horatio to thank him.

Then an elderly man in a dress suit and tie stumbled into the cavern. He carried Scarretchen's staff. "What's going on? How did this happen?" The sight of animals paired together seemed to enrage him. "Reunions are forbidden. There are no reunions in this life. Not in this world. Stop hugging." He strode over to the flying squirrels and broke them apart. "Stop it!" he shouted to two flickers—a husband and wife. He poked them away from each other with his staff.

"Could it be?" Horatio wondered. "Could this be Scarretchen himself?"

Scarretchen turned to Horatio. "How did you get out of your cage?" His voice softened. "Wait. Someone made a wish. Tell me! Is it true? Someone has a wishing stone. You!" he pointed to Horatio. The burnt-red stone lay in Horatio's paw. "You made a wish to free them, didn't you? That's a wishing stone, isn't it?" Horatio remained silent and closed his paw around the stone. "Isn't it!" Scarretchen shouted. "Give it to me! Give it to me!"

"Don't," cried Whisklet. "He'll undo everything you did."

"He'll turn us into worms or worse," shouted Whimser.

"No, no, I won't. I promise. Just let me have it." Scarretchen lunged for Horatio.

"Stop!" cried Leala. She aimed her arrow at him.

"I need it."

"Don't give it to him," said Whisklet. "You can't trust him. He can turn himself into anything he wants, remember? Even a pitiful old man."

"Please," Scarretchen said. "*Please*." His whole face had changed. He looked old and worn. His eyes seemed to have so much sadness in them. He no longer possessed the wild glare Horatio had seen in Scarretchen, the beast. "*Please*, I just need one more wish. I've only wanted one more wish." He stooped low and held out his wrinkled trembling hand in front of Horatio.

"Let's just get out of here," said Whimser. "While we can."

"Please, listen. I only need one more wish. I haven't been able to find a wishing stone for so many years. All I've needed is one more wish."

Horatio extended his paw to Scarretchen.

"*Horatio, don't!*" Whisklet screamed.

Horatio dropped the stone in Scarretchen's hand. "I know what wish he wants," he said.

Scarretchen's face lit up as he closed his fist around the

stone. His thick gray eyebrows raised up high. "It's getting warm! I can feel it! At last! At last!" An immense sense of relief came over his face. He closed his eyes, and with the most serene smile, he whispered a few words. Then he was gone. He had vanished.

In the stunned silence of the cavern, Horatio realized he no longer heard the sound of the river rushing inside him. Rollic was no longer calling to him. He went over to Rollic and hugged one of his white paws. "It's good to have you back," Horatio said softly.

For a brief moment, Horatio felt the warm calm of an embrace, as if it had been sent across the ocean on a breeze—the embrace of a father for his son, a husband for his wife, a family back together again.

"Where did Scarretchen go?" Whisklet asked. "What did he wish?"

Horatio sighed, "He wanted to go home."

Chapter 22

A Noble Thing

The creatures of the cavern streamed out of the tunnel into the bright light of day. They were free to go where their hearts' desired. For most that meant home. For Horatio and his gang—they were headed to the hedgehog village.

As they entered the woods outside the cave, they came upon a shrew dancing and singing, "I'm free! I'm free! I'm me! I'm me! The shrew that I was meant to be!"

"Honk! Honk!" Whimser laughed at the shrew's rhymes.

"Did you use to be a goose?" the shrew asked.

"Honk! No, not me."

"He just laughs like one," said Whisklet.

"I was going to say, if you had been a goose, you still have some in you."

"Honk! Honk!" Whimser started cracking everyone up. Rollic let out a low barking cough when he laughed, a cough Horatio hadn't heard before.

"Did you use to be the serpent?" asked Whisklet.

"That's right. I hated it. Now I'm me again. A simple shrew."

"Congratulations," Horatio told him, and shook his paw.

They said good-bye to the shrew and dashed through the forest to the beach, feeling nothing could stop them. But when they arrived at the beach, they discovered their raft had been carried out to sea. "I forgot about the tides," said Whisklet. The water was too deep. They had no way out by foot.

"I can carry you," said Rollic. "All of you."

All four small mammals clambered aboard Rollic. They each held on tight to his fur. Mish and Mosh climbed to the top of the Emblems to keep away from the salt water.

Rollic pushed off hard with his legs. The sea was choppy. Rollic panted hard.

"Are you all right?" Horatio asked.

"I'm getting my legs back. I haven't had otter legs for a long time."

Leala told Horatio all about Uncle Finneus and Aunt Quillity. "They thought you were killed by a hawk after you wandered off on your own. They've thought you were dead all these years."

Suddenly, Horatio realized he remembered his father and mother, and his brother too. "I have memories of my days in the village I didn't have before," said Horatio. "I remember shooting my bow and arrow with my dad. I remember the day my mother gave me this knapsack. I remember their faces." All sorts of memories flooded back to Horatio.

"Perhaps the wish you made changed you in some way. You can remember these things now," said Whisklet.

"Maybe I was always meant to remember them. But something made me forget. Leala, my brother was killed by a hawk—wasn't he?"

"That's right. It happened just a few weeks before you disappeared. Your parents thought they had lost both of their sons—one right after the other."

"That must have been terrible for them. I remember the day my brother was killed now. I was in the burrow, and my parents told me. I was too young to understand it fully. Did you tell my parents I'm alive?"

"No, I wanted to make sure you returned home safely before telling them anything. I didn't want their hearts to be broken again."

"They'll think I'm a ghost when they see me."

"Maybe at first. They'll probably recognize you. They'll certainly recognize your knapsack."

"But how did I end up so far north?"

"I have no idea how you ended up there. But your father came to the beach of wishing stones after your brother was killed. He didn't say what he wished for. But he thought his wish hadn't come true. That it really wasn't a wishing stone."

A sense of dismay came over Horatio. "They say when a wishing stone grants you a wish it takes something away. Maybe I was taken away." The feeling of dismay turned to alarm. "What was taken away from me, when I made my wish?" he wondered.

A strong wave splashed them. "Hold on," Rollic puffed.

"How are you doing, Rollic?"

"I don't know if I can make it."

"Just get us to the other side of the river," said Horatio. "None of us can swim very well."

Rollic hadn't realized how weak his legs had become. After having spent days as a moth, his whole body felt numb. The seawater made him shiver; the added weight of his companions on his back bore down on him.

Finally, Rollic reached the shore on the other side of the river. He dragged himself and his mates onto land. He was completely exhausted, and shivering from head to toe.

Leala kept an eye on Rollic, while the others hurried off to collect twigs and sticks. Whisklet got a roaring fire going.

They offered Rollic some berries and nuts from their knapsacks. He didn't eat them. They knew it wasn't the food for otters. But he drank some of their water, and with the heat of the fire, it seemed to soothe him a bit. His shivering stopped. Then he fell asleep. They watched his chest slowly rise and fall. He was still breathing.

"He doesn't look too good," said Whisklet. "He's going to need something more to eat."

Horatio wondered whether he should try to catch a fish for Rollic. He went over to Rollic, and lay on the ground so their faces were right next to each other. He held his paw. "Rollic," he whispered in his ear, "You're not going to die on me, are you? After I've come all this way?"

Rollic smiled, but didn't open his eyes. "I'm not going to die. I'm just going to sleep a bit."

"Okay, you sleep then."

Horatio gathered around the campfire along with the others. "He's just going to sleep." They felt the warm fire begin to dry out their clothes, still damp from the sea. Soon, Rollic was snoring loudly, a sound that put Horatio's mind more at ease.

"Everyone needs a home and a friend," said Horatio. "I felt I had both until Rollic disappeared."

"Rollic's not your only friend anymore," Whisklet told him. "You've got us now too."

"Thanks. I don't know what I would have done without you guys. I probably still would be tramping around some forest looking for a swimming hole."

Whisklet laughed. Whimser honked.

"Leala?" Horatio asked, "If my mother and father are your aunt and uncle, does that make us cousins?"

"No, they're not my real aunt and uncle. I just call

them that because they're like family."

"Oh," said Horatio. He thought for a moment. "Oh!" a broad smile swept over his face without him realizing it. Leala's ears turned bright pink.

Rollic's snoring now had become a high squeaky sound. It reminded Whisklet of Whimser's snake charmer. "Have you ever heard a finer performance on a snake charmer than the one we heard from Whimser today? Eeech! Eeech!" Whisklet mimicked. Whimser's ears turned pink now. But eventually Whisklet's imitation got a few honks out of Whimser.

Then Rollic let out a low moan that seemed to ache with pain. "He's going to need nourishment," said Leala.

"He eats fish." Horatio glanced over at his friend. "I could catch a fish with my bow and arrow. Do you think it's wrong to kill a fish, if it's just swimming in the water, not bothering anyone?"

"I don't know," said Leala. "I'm not sure how otters would survive without fish."

"Then is it wrong for the hawks to eat hedgehogs?"

"I don't think the hawks feel it's wrong. They probably feel as if they're just doing what they were born to do—they eat small mammals. But I've seen the pain it causes. Too many families have lost a loved one."

Rollic moaned again in his sleep. "Do fish have families?" Horatio asked. "Mish and Mosh, have you ever spoken to a fish?"

"Well," said Mosh, "we're much more fluent in

shellfish." He pointed his head toward his shell. "We haven't had many chancesh to talk to a fish, though. We don't shpend time underwater."

"We did talk to a fish who had beached himshelf on land once," said Mish. "He wash pretty weak."

"What did he say?"

'Water.' That'sh the lasht word he shaid."

Rollic let out another long moan. "He seems to be getting worse," said Horatio. Horatio stood up. He took out the rope from his knapsack and cut off a piece with his pocketknife. Then he tied the rope to one of his arrows. "Mosh, you come with me."

Horatio walked down to the water. He looked behind at Mosh, but he didn't seem to be moving. Then he looked away, and Mosh quickly caught up with him.

Horatio stood on a rock, and waited until he saw a fish swim by. He aimed his arrow and fired. The arrow lodged into the side of the fish. He pulled the fish up out of the water onto the shore. The fish flopped about with the arrow stuck in him.

"Tell him he's doing a noble thing," said Horatio to Mosh. "He's saving another life."

Mosh walked over to the fish and spoke to him. The fish's mouth moved a few times and then he died.

"What did he say?"

"He shaid he never *wanted* to be noble."

Horatio stood there, stunned. Tears came to his eyes. "I've never spoken to a fish before. I shouldn't have killed him. Maybe this fish had a friend, a friend who'll search everywhere for him, like I searched for Rollic. But his friend will never find him."

Mosh glided up Horatio's right arm to his shoulder, and whispered, "You've been through a lot. You're jusht trying to shave Rollic."

Horatio wiped the tears away. "I'm not trying to *shave* him, you silly snail." The tears came back. "Maybe there's only so much you can do, or should do, even for a friend." Horatio knelt down next to the fish. "I never wanted to be noble, either." He grasped the arrow and pulled it out. "I'm sorry."

Whisklet and Whimser came down to help bring the fish back. "We're not going to drag him," Horatio told them, as he turned his head and wiped the tears off again. They lifted the fish onto their shoulders. Whisklet took the head. Horatio and Whimser took the tail. They brought the fish back to Rollic.

Horatio put the fish near Rollic's head. He whispered in Rollic's ear, "I brought you a fish."

Rollic's eyes opened and he smiled again. He rested his head against the fish as if it were a pillow. "That smells good. Thanks pal. I think I'll save it for later." He went back to sleep.

Horatio remembered their long-standing joke. Rollic never saved anything for later.

Chapter 23

The Reunion

They sat around the fire waiting for some sign that Rollic might recover.

"Horatio," Whisklet said gently, "why don't you and Leala go ahead to your village? We'll look after Rollic."

"No," Horatio said. "I'll wait here."

Whisklet spoke even more gently to him, "What do you think was taken away from you when you made your wish?" He glanced over at Rollic.

Horatio's face turned white. He raised a paw and pointed a claw at Whisklet, "That's not going to happen." Horatio's whole body shook. "Do you hear me? Rollic's going to eat that fish and he's going to get better."

Night fell. The small mammals decided to sleep around

the fire rather than dig a burrow. Mish and Mosh made up their own minds to take turns staying awake through the night. Someone had to keep an eye out.

In the middle of the night, Horatio dreamed he heard Rollic's chomping, gulping, and slurping sounds. Then he dreamed some slime was dripping down his face. He rubbed it. The sensation of slime roused him from his dream. "Horatio," he heard a voice whisper. He opened his eyes to see Mosh on his forehead peering down at him. "Look!" Horatio sat up. Rollic was eating the fish!

"Rollic!" Horatio cried.

"This fish is *good*. Thanks. I feel the life coming back in me." He chomped and slurped some more.

Horatio shook his head, "We weren't sure if we were going to get you back."

Whisklet, Whimser, and Leala had now awakened. They all came over to Rollic to pat him on the head. In the light of the fire, they could see his black nose go up and down in appreciation.

"I'm feeling more and more like me again," he said, taking the last bites of fish.

They stayed up the rest of the night. They talked about what it felt like to be a moth, what Rollic's parents would say when they saw him. How Horatio felt Scarretchen really was reunited with his family now, but Horatio couldn't say what the wishing stone had taken away from Scarretchen when it granted his wish.

"What do you think the wishing stone took away from

me?" Horatio asked. No one could answer him. "I hope my wish didn't do any harm."

As the morning set in, the group let the fire die out, and set off for Horatio's village once more. Horatio and Leala walked ahead on the sandy shore, with Rollic behind them, and Whisklet and Whimser in the rear. Mish and Mosh both rode atop Whimser's knapsack now, so Horatio and Leala could talk.

"How did you find us?"

"I had climbed up the same tree Mish and Mosh climbed. I couldn't see you down below because of the fog. I was going to call to your snail friends, but then Scarretchen came out. I couldn't believe how fast those snails got back down that tree."

"But how did you cross the river?"

"I used a sea tortoise, just as your dad did when he made the trip."

"What are my parents like now?"

"Your dad's still an explorer. He was a champion archer. Do you remember that? So was my dad."

"I remember him as an archer, but I don't think I really knew he was an explorer. What's my mom like now?"

"Your mom's not in the best of health. But she still knits. She made this quiver for me before the tournament."

"The letters on your quiver are similar to those on my knapsack," said Horatio. "But I never would have guessed they were made by the same person."

Horatio glanced at Leala, not sure if he should say what

he was thinking. "Leala," Horatio said quietly, "I think my dad's wish took me away from the village. Maybe it took my memories of the village too. I wonder what he wished for."

"I asked him, but he wouldn't say. Only that he wished it had come true."

I can't imagine how they'll react when they see me."

"It will be the best day of their lives," said Leala.

In the distance, Horatio and Leala could see two small figures on the shore heading toward them. They were both hedgehogs, and they both carried a bow and quiver of arrows.

"Horatio," Leala whispered to him, "that's my dad on the right, and yours on the left. They must have headed out to look for me."

They began to come into clearer view. "Leala!" her father, Wal, called. They rushed to meet each other. "Where have you been?" He gave her a great hug.

"I went to help Horatio."

Finneus and Wal stared curiously at him. "Where are you from?"

"Do you recognize the knapsack?" Leala asked.

Finneus nodded. "It was my boy's knapsack. Where did you find it?"

"I've always had it," said Horatio. "It's never left me."

Finneus stared more closely at Horatio, something in the young hedgehog's eyes, his shy smile, was familiar. "Horatio?" he whispered as if talking to someone he wasn't sure was there. "Is it you?" Horatio smiled. Finneus knew that smile. "Oh, my boy! It is you!" He hugged him. "Oh, my boy!"

As they walked back to the village, Horatio turned to his father, "Dad?" Finneus hadn't been called that in years. He put his arm around Horatio."What did you wish for when you went to the wishing stones?"

"It was a simple wish.The kind of wish any father might wish for his son. It was a few weeks after your brother was killed by a hawk. I couldn't bear the thought of losing you. I just wished for you to be safe. How I wished it had come true."

Then it became clear to Horatio. That was why no predators ever bothered him when he lived in his burrow by the riverbank. That's why the hawk that attacked him, had dropped him. Why Scarretchen couldn't turn him into a roach. His father's wish had protected him.

"Your wish did come true, Dad. I've been safe all these years."

Horatio entered his family's burrow with his father.

"Quillity?" Finneus called to her softly.

"Yes?" she called back from her bed.

Finneus stayed at the doorway. He didn't go to her bedroom. "The most amazing thing has happened."

"Did you find Leala?"

"Yes."

"Thank goodness."

"But something even more amazing has happened. We found someone else." Finneus nodded to Horatio.

Horatio stepped into Quillity's bedroom. "Hi, Mom. It's me."

"Horatio?" Was she dreaming, she wondered. She looked at him as if she were seeing an angel.

Finneus came into the bedroom too. When he saw Quillity's face he didn't know what to say. He raised his shoulders in one splendid, wordless shrug.

She saw Horatio's knapsack and extended her arms to him. "This isn't a dream!" Horatio bent over and hugged his mother. "Horatio!"

The whole village gathered outside for another celebration. They decided to hold it outside rather than in the social hall, so Rollic could be there. The Emblems of Graysent were prominently displayed. Quillity insisted on getting out of bed and joining the celebration too.

Horatio couldn't believe all the hedgehogs around him. Many of them remembered him from when he was a little boy. "It's a miracle," Horatio heard over and over.

He didn't know what to make of it all. But he felt right at home. He felt he was where he belonged.

❧

Rollic's parents and his brother swam down the river to meet Rollic. The Wingwots had told them Rollic was safe in the hedgehog village. Rollic's parents weren't angry at him this time for not getting home before dark. Horatio had never seen so many otters wiggle and shake in happiness.

"Good-bye," Horatio gave Rollic another hug. "Visit often."

"We will," said Rollic. "It's a lot easier for otters to swim downriver than for hedgehogs to hike up it." Horatio laughed.

Whisklet and Whimser needed to get home too.

"Thank you," said Horatio. "I couldn't have rescued Rollic and found my family without you. Graysent will be proud of you. You carried the Emblems well."

"We wouldn't have made it without *you*," said Whisklet.

"I'll never forget the shot you made to save us from the waterfall," said Whimser.

"Good-bye, Mish and Mosh." Horatio patted them on their shells.

"Thish wash the besht adventure ever," said Mosh. Mish nodded in agreement.

"I'm going to miss you guys," said Horatio. "I wish, I

mean, it would be nice if we didn't live so far apart."

Later that afternoon, after Horatio's friends had left for their homes, Leala and Horatio walked to the beach. "I think I know what my wish took away from me," Horatio told Leala. "It took away my father's protection. I was never meant to live a sheltered life by myself in a burrow. That wasn't who I was meant to be. I'd rather live here in my home with you and my family, even in a world where I could be attacked by hawks, than live in a protected world alone.

"In some ways I'm more on my own than ever. There's no magical protection to keep me safe. There's no way of knowing what's going to happen next or how it might turn out. It could be fun or scary. But I wouldn't want it any other way."

Horatio and Leala lay in the sand, feeling the sun warm their bellies and the cool ocean water gently lap their toes. The summer weather almost always seemed agreeable to Horatio. He felt a slight nibble on his toes under the water. "A little fish?" he wondered.

CPSIA information can be obtained at www.ICGtesting.com
Printed in the USA
LVOW10s1604150813

348092LV00017B/594/P